THE LONG SILK LINE

Dr. Wendell Zehel

THE LONG SILK LINE

Dr. Wendell Zehel

Sterling House Publishers
Pittsburgh, PA

Sterling House Paperback

ISBN 1-156315-077-8

© Copyright 1998 Wendell Zehel
All rights reserved
First Printing—1998

Request for information should be addressed to:

Sterling House Publisher
The Sterling Building
440 Friday Road
Pittsburgh, PA 15209

Cover design & Typesetting: Drawing Board Studios

All rights reserved. No part of this publication may be reproduced, stored in a retrieval system, or transmitted in any form or by any means—electronic, mechanical, photocopy, recording or any other, except for brief quotations in printed reviews—without prior permission of the publisher.

Printed in the United States of America

Dedicated
to Dr. John D. Meyers, MD

1

D<small>R. J</small>OSHUA W<small>ALKER</small> sat down on a park bench next to his friend Walt. "Here, want half my breakfast biscuit? It's Canadian bacon and Swiss. Very good." Josh held out the sandwich, but Walt made no move to accept it.

"Naw. Thanks, though." Walt shook his head. They'd met for breakfast, but Walt wasn't eating. Josh knew why: Walt had been laid off from his post at the steel mill in '74, just a year ago, and now he had just lost his sale's job at an electronics store.

Josh gazed out over the wide river valley, golden in the light of dawn. It was almost pretty, now that so many mills were closed or operating at low capacity, thought Josh. Then he realized what that meant to Walt and closed his eyes in shame. He took a bite of food, but it was tasteless. "What's the matter? You can get another job."

Walt nodded. "True. But not in the mills. It'll never come back. It'll never be the same." He let out a long, sad sigh. "Some of the guys who are still working think that the layoffs are temporary, that management is just trying to fool the union into backing off on their demands. I don't believe that, though."

Josh rummaged though the brown bag he had got from the deli. "I have an orange. Would you like it?"

"No, thanks."

"What happened? At Tronic World, I mean."

Walt shrugged and tossed a crushed soda cracker to a pair of smog-colored pigeons at his feet. "I don't know for sure. They said they were laying off "excess personnel." Don't know how I got the job in the first place. You know I'm not much of an office person. Guess that applies to sales, too."

Josh knew what Walt meant. He had been friends with Walt since high school, and even then Walt could not handle any kind of rules, restraints, schedules or protocol. He lived for weekends when he could ride his Harley Davidson, whenever Providence provided gasoline.

After high school, before his father got him a job at the mill, Walt had gotten himself into trouble, breaking into dime stores and stealing candy and cigarettes. It had been the challenge, not the loot, that made him do it, Josh knew. Gradually he had become more and more careless until even the police were able to track him down. Maybe the people at Tronic World had gotten hold of Walt's criminal records.

"Look at that," Walt said, nodding toward the traffic at the edge of the park. "Do you realize that every one of those people is driving a Honda or a Subaru or a Toyota?"

"Not every one, I'm sure." Josh looked up at the blur of cars; he couldn't tell one from the other, but Walt had a talent for that sort of thing. He almost said that he drove a Volvo, then decided against it, even though it was 10 years old.

"Well, okay," Walt snorted. "I just seems that Americans are using so many things from other countries these days. I mean, whatever happened to buying American?"

Josh shrugged. "Our products aren't as good?" he ventured. "Or as inexpensive?"

"Bingo," Walt said. "Guess I don't blame anyone for trying to get good value. Our stuff is crap compared to what it used to be. People used to take pride in their work, you know? Now even people in the factories don't give a damn about how well they do something. My brother's in Detroit. He tells me most of the automotive workers would just as soon glue the chassis together if they thought they could get away with it."

He paused and threw another piece of cracker at the persistent birds. "Ain't it funny about life, though?" he continued, his voice a steady monotone. "National Steel moved the plant to Korea because of cheaper labor. We steelworkers and the union just priced ourselves out of jobs, but Hell! We worked hard. We deserved to make more."

Josh searched his mind for a distraction. Walt was just too depressed—and depressing. He was sure Walt wasn't in any danger, not just yet, at any rate, but mulling over his losses was preventing him from really living. "See the wife and kids lately?"

"No." Walt shook his head, staring at the pigeons. "Pam and the girls went to live with her parents last year. She just couldn't put up with me anymore, even for short visits. Too depressing, she said."

"Well, at least you still have the house."

"Wrong-o." Walt finally turned to gaze into Josh's face, and Josh saw a great depth of sadness in the man's eyes. "The bank took it two months ago. Nothing's left."

Walt turned back toward the valley. "I can remember when this place was filled with smoke every day. People went to and fro to work...all that hustle and bustle! Now look at it. It's almost like a God-damned cemetery, like someone dropped a bomb on all those people. And it's only going to get worse."

"Well, things change," Josh said, wincing the moment his words were out of his mouth. It was a stupid thing to say, so obvious. And that change wasn't necessarily for the better, either. Walt and hundreds of others had been hurt, almost destroyed by it.

"I've got some savings," Josh tried again. "I can put you up in a hotel or The Y for a while, and when you get another job, you can find a place of your own." Even as he spoke, he knew he was talking nonsense.

"Thanks but no thanks," Walt murmured, still staring into the valley. "My sister's putting me up for a while. That is, unless the Japanese buy her house and force me out. Don't worry about me. I'll get by." Walt turned to Josh and looked up at him as if he hadn't seen him until that very moment. "Say, don't you look great!" He nodded at Josh's blue suit and trim haircut and gave a half-hearted smile.

Josh laughed. For a moment, he had seen the old Walt, the sly court jester who could not take life seriously. "You're only just noticing? These are the first real clothes I've bought since I left the army."

"Well, you do look like a real person," Walt murmured thoughtfully, "not some career-army dude. What's up? Trying to impress a new girlfriend?"

"In a way," Josh answered. "My residency at St. Cahill's hospital starts today."

Josh checked his watch. "In about half an hour, in fact."

Josh hated to leave Walt, but he had to go: He had a meeting with Dr. Thornton, the chief of surgery, at 10:00. The morning marked a new beginning for him, and a another dead end for Walt. Josh laid his hand on his friend's shoulder, and the man's eyes flickered briefly. "You need any help, you know where to reach me," he said. He rose, scattering the pigeons as he did so, and left half a sandwich and the orange in the bench. "I mean it."

Walt nodded. His eyes were blank again but a faint smile still curled on his lips. "I know you do. Thanks for coming by. It means a lot."

Josh walked down the hill to the parking lot, turning back now and then to look at Walt, but his friend didn't budge. When he reached his car, Josh climbed in and drove off, without another backward glance. He couldn't help Walt unless Walt wanted help, he told himself. But even so he felt as if he had just suffered some tremendous disappointment or failure. It was a stupid thought for a man about to begin a promising new enterprise, he reminded himself, but there it was, anyway, and it was not easy to shake.

The city looked beautiful as he drove over a sweeping bridge toward the South Side. The tall buildings of downtown glimmered in the distance in the early summer sunshine. Ahead of him, St. Cahill's Hospital held a commanding position on a hill above the adjacent community, like a feudal fortress. It was an imposing Gothic structure, its white brick tower jutting forward, as if in self-confidence, over the rivers, highways and sprawling network of city houses.

Josh tried to remember what he had read and heard about the hospital from his future colleagues. It was operated by the local university, which treated indigent patients, but had a separate, private section—the Gold Coast, the staff called it—for the wealthier clientele. The chairmen of the various departments at St. Cahill's were in charge of vast medical conglomerates, which gave them enormous power in the medical world. Josh knew he would have to tread warily among these worthies.

Still, he was thrilled about the prospect of working at St. Cahill's. More than the honor of training at such a prestigious facility, Josh valued the chance to find out what it was really like to work in a hospital—all the dimensions of professional medicine, the good and the bad. He was looking forward to the challenge as much as to the excitement of being part of St. Cahill's, the opportunity to work with some of the legends of modern surgery, especially Dr. Thornton, the chief of surgery. Josh imagined himself at Thornton's side, drinking in the man's expertise. It was an uplifting image.

Parking his car in the hospital garage, Josh entered St. Cahill's lobby and approached the receptionist, who sat, bored and sleepy-looking, at a large circular desk. "Excuse me, can you direct me to the Department of Surgery?" he asked.

"Oh, the war office," she said curtly. "We'll have someone come and show you the way."

The war office? Josh thought. Did they couch everything in military terms? He had just spent five years as a doctor with the army, and wasn't sure he wanted to go back to such rigid regimentation.

After a short wait, Josh saw Sperling Nelson, the chief resident on the first surgical service, turn a corner and approach him. He remembered the muscular, fair-haired man from an earlier visit. Nelson's bright blue eyes lit up in recognition and his handsome face burst into a white smile. "Glad to see you again, Dr. Walker," he said, grabbing Josh's hand in a powerful grip. "The surgical service is short staffed, so your presence is doubly welcome. There are no medical students here in the summer, of course, and we need all the help we can get."

Nelson's warm greeting reassured Josh. The surgeon made him feel wanted, needed, confident that he would not be considered just another small working part of a large, complicated machine.

"Plan on staying a while?"

Josh nodded. "Yes, I discussed that with the chief. He assured me I would be here at least a year."

"At least a year," Nelson repeated. For some reason he couldn't name, Josh's confidence began to fade. Somehow Nelson made him feel as if the prospect of lasting a year at St. Cahill's was a remote possibility.

"Well, keep your eyes open," Nelson said. "You'll meet a lot of interesting personalities here. Very interesting."

Before he could wonder what Nelson meant, the surgeon hustled Josh into an elevator and took him the surgeon's quarters on the twelfth floor. As they began walking down a hallway, they passed a short, dark doctor with his head bowed, staring straight at the floor. "Dr. Walker, this is Dr. John Ravis, assistant chief of surgery," Nelson said.

Ravis raised his head an inch or so, glanced at Josh and snorted as he passed. He didn't stop, or even slow down. "Not in a very good mood today, I guess," Josh murmured. As a resident, he expected to get little respect from established doctors, but Ravis's rebuff still rankled him.

"Well, he's got a good reason," Nelson replied. "The tenure committee turned down his application yesterday. He has one more year to make tenure or he's out. Guess I'd be pretty pissed off, too."

Josh looked up at Nelson, surprised by the crude remark. "Why was he denied tenure?" he asked. "Do you know?"

"You never can tell," Nelson said, holding one half of a

double door open for Josh. "Getting tenure around here is tougher than believing the Penguins will win the Stanley Cup. And once you get washed out of the system, you have no place to go." He chuckled, though Josh found nothing amusing about the statement.

Nelson ushered Josh into the suite of small rooms that comprised the residents' quarters. The halls and doors were all painted pale green, and, though everything was clean and neat, the hall smelled like cigarette smoke and had the sad look of a corridor in a cheap hotel. "Dr. Walker, you'll do just fine here," Nelson said. "Just do what I tell you and everything will be A-OK."

Josh frowned, annoyed by Nelson's inability to call him by just one name, and worried by the veiled threat in the doctor's last words. He and Nelson walked to his room, a small cubicle with a metal cot, a sink and one window covered by mini-blinds. There was no air conditioning, Josh noted with some chagrin, but a phone had been placed strategically next to the bed.

"Don't worry about the lack of air conditioning," Nelson said. "The only time you'll ever see that bed is at night, if you're lucky. You'll get a cool breeze up here in the evening, and it's always nice and quiet. The only residents who use the quarters during the day are the eyeball specialists. I guess they need their rest after a tiring morning of eye exams."

They left the residents' quarters, and Nelson took Josh on a tour of the hospital—the emergency suite, the operating rooms, the teaching theater, and ambulatory care facilities. Nelson was about to show Josh the new geriatric care unit when Josh noticed the time. "It's almost 10:30," he said, "and I have a meeting with Thornton at 11:00. Maybe another time."

"Thornton?" Nelson's eyebrows rose to just below his neatly trimmed bangs. "Dr. Thaddeus J. Thornton, III. You know about him, don't you?"

Josh cocked his head. What did Nelson mean? "Everyone has heard of Dr. Thornton and the Thornton Technique for bypass surgery. I met him when I was here before, but we didn't get a chance to discuss his work at St. Cahill's very much, if that's what you're getting at."

"Thornton's a product of the `Long Silk Line,' and he's damn proud of it," Nelson muttered.

Josh nodded; he'd heard of the long silk line throughout his training. The group of prominent surgical professors from John's Hopkins University had been founded by William Halstead, a pioneer of modern surgical procedures, including aseptic surgical techniques. He's been the very first to use rubber gloves in the operating room. "Man, that would be the opportunity of a lifetime, wouldn't it? To participate in a program like that. I've read a lot of Halstead's works. I guess you could say he's my hero."

Nelson gave Josh a shifty look, as if he were about to smile and had thought better of it. "Might be more useful to read Machiavelli around here," he muttered.

"What?"

"Nothing." Nelson adjusted his jacket, which had needed no adjustment. "Thornton's a prince, no doubt about it. Came from Baltimore via one of the great medical facilities in New York. His specialty is vascular surgery, particularly portal caval shunts and heart valve replacements. Around here, a lot of people just call him Dr. God."

Josh imagined the chief wearing a golden halo, holding a magic scepter in his right hand. With one flick of the scepter, Thornton could command the dead to rise and walk. Probably talks with God on a daily basis, Josh thought, suddenly flooded by a deep sense of his own inferiority. But what had Nelson meant about Machiavelli?

"Daydreaming, Walker?" Nelson snapped. "You'd better hurry if you want to freshen up before you visit with the big man. I'll meet you there, with the other residents."

Josh stopped in the surgeon's lounge to wash his face. As he stared into the tiny mirror above the sink, he fancied himself a future famous chief of surgery at some well-known institute or prestigious hospital. Despite the odd feeling he'd gotten from

Nelson, he felt sure that great things lay ahead of him, and that this renowned institution was his path to a glorious future.

He slicked back his hair, moistened his lips, and tried to evaluate his appearance in the mirror. Walt had been right: His blue suit made him look like a "real person," not a military flunky. It gave him a clean-cut, preppy look that a chief of surgery might look on with approval.

Josh reached Thornton's office with five minutes to spare and ran into a group of older fellows in Thornton's outer office. Nelson was there, along with Dr. Dan Bloomstein, the chief resident on the second surgical service. He had arrived months ago from the Mayo Clinic, according to Nelson, and several members of the department looked down on him: They considered Mayo's training program to be inferior to St. Cahill's. Several junior residents were there, including Lois Dorsinger, who was studying plastic surgery. Even now, in fairly liberated times, Josh thought it was odd to see a female resident, since the field of surgery was still widely thought of—in private, at least—as the domain of the macho white male physician.

Eileen, the chief's pretty, blonde secretary, greeted the residents graciously with kind words and ushered them into the chief's office.

Thornton was a heavy-set, tall man with thinning sandy-colored hair and a tight smile that made Josh feel a little uneasy. The chief asked everyone to sit down, then launched into a welcoming address, probably the one he used every year, thought Josh.

"Welcome aboard, doctors. It's a pleasure to have you in this training program. Keep in mind it's not just a surgical training program, you know. It's training for all you'll do in life. You'll find companionship and camaraderie here that you won't find anywhere else in the world. But let's get one thing straight: This is serious business. There's no time for playing around."

Thornton's voice was deep and commanding. Josh felt a chill race though him as the chief continued. Words poured from him like the commands of a general at the head of a charging infantry line.

"Breakfast at 6:00 a.m. in the cafeteria. Rounds start promptly at 7:00. Intakes, fluid outlays and vital signs should be available on all patients. The O.R. schedule starts promptly at 8:00. The junior resident will ensure that the patient is prepared for surgery and will write all post-op orders. Dressing rounds begin in the afternoon after surgery. Teaching rounds follow. Grand rounds at 4:00 p.m. on Tuesdays and Fridays. Junior residents are on call at all times, in the house every other night. When they are not in the house, they will carry a beeper. The chief resident will be available at all times for any problems with patients on his service." He paused for a moment, and Josh thought he could hear the loud silence that suddenly filled the office. "Any questions?"

Josh's head was spinning. He felt intimidated, as insignificant as a sparrow in the talons of a falcon.

"As you know," Thornton went on, his voice still pulsating with command, "the staff has been given a hefty raise to $400 a month. No laundry, no moonlighting. If anyone is caught moonlighting, they'll be fired immediately. One last thing, and hear this loud and clear: There is to be no sexual contact with the medical students, nursing staff, or other residents. Male or female. Familiarity breeds contempt. Do I make myself clear?"

Josh shook his head in bewilderment. If Moses had stepped into the office to deliver the Ten Commandments, Josh thought, he couldn't have made a bigger impression than Dr. God. He looked around the room and saw people shaking their heads in confusion, muttering to each other. Doubtless they didn't agree with Thornton's demands, but Josh thought the chief was right on the mark. He remembered something his father had said to him years ago, when Josh was just beginning to notice that girls were an altogether different and intriguing type of being. "Josh, there's nothing that can distract a man from his work more completely than a pretty woman," the old man had said. "You've got a job to do, boy, and until you do it, don't let the urge to procreate stand in your way, so to speak."

Apparently Dr. Thornton held the same beliefs as Josh's dad, and Josh admired him for that. Josh had no girlfriend at the moment, and he didn't intend to look for one, either. He could court only one sweetheart at a time, and right now his career was his only mistress.

"One more thing," the chief continued. "We like to see papers. The first year resident should have one completed by the end of the year. You will not become a chief resident until you publish three or four papers in major medical journals. We've been considering a pyramid system...you know, a system in which we start with four first-year residents and end up with one chief resident in the fourth year. But, due to financial limitations and administrative considerations, that project may not get off the ground this year."

Josh felt his head turning from side to side in dumbfoundment, as if he had no control over his disbelief. Thornton's system couldn't possibly work. How could anyone learn the trade *and* write scholarly papers when he was more exhausted and dispirited than a Chinese cooley? How could anyone develop a spirit of innovative, creative thinking when caught up in a lockstep regime that prized efficiency over individual excellence?

Thornton spewed out a few pleasantries, as if to smooth over the brutality of his earlier instructions, then unceremoniously left the office without a word of explanation. As the other residents stirred themselves from their stupor and began to file out of the room, Josh found himself rooted to his seat. He had hoped to come to St. Cahill's to solve at least some of the problems of humanity; now, instead, he was squarely involved in problems of his own.

As Josh left the chief's office, he found Nelson waiting for him in the hall. "Dr. Walker, I'll round up the intern and resident and meet you on Three East in fifteen minutes. There are two assistants around here somewhere who should also make rounds with us."

Josh nodded, struggling to make sense of Nelson's instructions. He was still recovering from the chief's barrage of instructions and attempting to regain his composure, but to do so was like struggling with a migraine headache that wasn't responding to medication. He thought of Walt and wished he too lived for a cold beer and 90 miles an hour on a chopper on a straightaway in the country.

When Josh arrived on Three East, he introduced himself to the ward clerk, Linda Sommers. A friendly young woman with long brown hair and hazel eyes, she gave Josh a wide smile, exposing sparkling white teeth.

Josh returned the smile with a gracious nod as he began thumbing through the charts she handed him. Some were quite voluminous, as if the patient had been in the hospital for ages.

"Have you seen the intern or the junior student?" he asked Linda.

"No, Dr. Walker. I couldn't find the medical student, but the intern will be here shortly."

"And Dr. Nelson."

Linda glanced at the floor. "Probably in the nurse's lounge. Candy, you know."

Josh cocked his head. "Candy? You mean from vending machines?"

She sighed and shook her head. "No, Candace Bach, the

head nurse. They're...chummy. Boy, doctor, you do have a lot to learn."

Josh stared at the ward clerk, about to stutter something about Dr. Thornton and his "no intimacy" regulations, when the chubby intern and the harried-looking junior student jogged up to him. "Help me wheel the chart rack into the ward," Josh barked at them. "Time's a'wastin'."

The ward consisted of a large, partitioned room with sixteen beds in the center of the wing, and six single room further down the hall. Approaching the first patient, Mr. Brody, Josh mentally examined him from head to toe. The chart showed that the man had been admitted with a recurrent inguinal hernia.

"Doc, what's wrong with me?" asked Brody, as Josh removed the sheet from the man's chest and scarred belly and began his physical examination. Josh tried to explain, but Brody interrupted him. "Yeah, yeah...I *know* it's a hernia. But this will be the third time I've had it repaired. Why does it keep coming back? Why can't you guys fix it for good?"

Josh replaced the sheet, pulled up a chair and began answering the man's questions. They were good questions, and deserved some explanations. "The muscle tissue might be weakened by the extensive surgery, Mr. Brody," he said, "or perhaps you have inadvertently strained the suture site."

As he kept talking, the intern, Dr. Willowby, kept glancing at his watch. At last he laid his hand on Josh's shoulder. "Dr. Walker, we have to continue our rounds. We have a very limited amount of time for each patient."

Josh scowled up at Willowby, irritated that the young man would even attempt to deprive his patient of important information. "Mr. Brody wants some answers to his concerns, Dr. Willowby. And while we're at it, I have a question for you: Who devised the very first hernia repair?"

The intern's pasty face grew tense as he struggled for an answer. "Uh, Bassini?" he gulped at last.

Josh glared at the intern's trembling double chin. Steve Willowby was young and solid now, but if left to graze on his own after the rigors of residency, he would end up decidedly fat.

"What sort of an answer is that? Where did you train, anyway?"

"Wrong answer, Dr. Walker?" Willowby asked.

Josh snorted and shook his head. "Dr. William Halstead, that's who. This is the long silk line, remember?"

Willowby shrugged. "Okay, sir. Walking in Dr. God's footsteps, eh, Dr. Walker?"

"Now you've got the picture," Josh said, frowning. "So what else can you tell me about Mr. Brody's current condition?"

"Well, we're still waiting for medical clearance, doctor," Willowby answered softly.

Josh sensed that Willowby had something else to say, so he reassured Mr. Brody as best he could, promised to get back to him with more information, and finished up his physical exam. Back out in the hall he took Willowby aside. "What's were you saying about medical clearance for this patient?" Josh asked. "Is there a problem?"

"Well, medical service is awfully slow. They want some more workup on his heart."

"What?" snapped Josh, thumbing through the chart. "This patient has already gone through two surgeries. Just what type of workup do they need?"

Dr. Willowby leaned close. "Geez, doctor," he said under his breath, "the medical department will have him undergo every test conceivable before they order a medical clearance. *If* then."

"Ridiculous!" snorted Josh. Obviously the medical service had some sort of rivalry going with the medical staff. He felt his face grow warm with anger. "This in inexcusable."

"You're telling me." Willowby rolled his eyes in resignation. "God, sometimes it takes them a week just to see a consult, and then another two weeks to sort out all the tests. It's a mess, if you ask me."

Josh sighed, determined not to let the debacle with the medical service ruin his rounds. He worked his way through the rest of the patients in the large room and was starting down the hall, on his way to the single rooms, when Nelson came up to him, all smiles.

"Have a nice snack?" Josh muttered sarcastically, but Nelson only nodded as the little group made its way to the first room. "Room 18, Mr. Dantell," Nelson said with authority. He'd obviously memorized all the patients in the order they were lined up for surgery. "His right colon has a blockage, which we'll remove in the morning."

Josh looked at the patient and had to suppress a gasp. At first glance, Dantell reminded him of his father as he had appeared shortly before his death. The cancer had wasted his dad's body until he was hardly more substantial than a child, and Dantell was similarly weak and wasted. His skin, stretched tight over his protuberant belly, looked taut and shiny. "Dr. Nelson, how much of a bowel prep has the patient had?" he asked.

"Not much, Dr. Walker. Unfortunately, he is almost totally obstructed."

"Maybe he should be decompressed first."

The patient looked up at Nelson. "Doc, do you think everything will be okay?" he asked, his voice marked by a noticeable quiver.

"You can bet on it," Nelson answered, almost jovial. "Just leave the driving to us." His eyes glimmered as he lightly touched the man's distended abdomen.

Dantell shivered in pain. Josh took the man's hand and gripped it firmly, convinced that Nelson's flippant tone was nothing but swagger. "Mr. Dantell, you know this is serious surgery, but we're going to do our best, and our best is very good. I'll be right with you all the way, and if you have any questions, you can ask me."

Josh suddenly felt uneasy, remembering that a doctor had said something very similar to Josh's father days before he died on the operating table. But what else could he do or say? It was his first day on the job. Nelson frowned, and they quickly finished their exam and left. "Doctor, you can't be too direct with the patients," Nelson warned. "Dantell's going to be fine. You should have let it go at that."

Josh reluctantly agreed. After all, Nelson had more experience in these matters that he did. His cheerful manner had probably helped a lot of patients. As he continued his rounds, Josh almost forgot Dantell, and his doubts quickly dissipated.

They were almost finished with the ward work when Josh was called to the emergency room. The place was a scene of orderly chaos as nurses and doctors rushed back and forth tending to six or seven bleeding people, including two children. An auto accident which had killed both drivers had left all seven passengers with severe lacerations of the face and head. One woman had a bad gash on her hand, and one traumatized young man was screaming in terror.

In contrast, the two children, both under ten years old, were silent, paralyzed by shock and fear.

Josh approached the younger child, a girl about six. "I'm Dr. Walker," he said quietly, patting the girl's blonde head. "I'm going to help you, and I'm going to give you something to make you go to sleep so it doesn't hurt. Okay?"

The terrified child stared up at him, her eyes perfectly round. "Go to sleep like the kittens?" she said through bleeding lips.

Josh was bewildered for a moment, then he understood. "No, honey, you'll wake up, and you'll get better. All right?" The girl gave one swift nod. He grinned, then turned away from her. "Anesthesia," he barked to a nurse.

For the next two hours, Josh labored over the two children and three of the adults. Nelson saw to the others. The suture work was tricky and exhausting, and to make matters worse, the injured man kept on screaming, despite a massive dose of Demerol. When Josh finally had a chance to look at his watch, it was eight o'clock.

"Wonderful work, Dr. Walker," said the head nurse, patting him on the shoulder. "I don't know when I've ever seen such good hands before. Believe me, when these people realize what you've done for them, they'll kiss your feet. Uh...and your hands." She smiled.

"I just wish they'd buy me dinner," Josh laughed. Although he felt as if he hadn't eaten in days, he was too exhilarated to care. This was what St. Cahill's stood for, he thought—the best medical staff, doing the best work possible under severe pressure. It was about comforting children, soothing tortured adults and healing serious wounds. They could do it. They had done it. It was great: He and the others had made a difference. Despite the fact that he thought he might fall to the ground with weariness at any moment, Josh was ready to do it all again.

It wasn't long before his hunger began to get his undivided attention. He hurried to the dining room as soon as he could, but it was closed. "Damn!" He'd been looking forward to a hot meal. Josh considered finding a restaurant in the area, then decided to settle for a sandwich from the little coffee shop in the lower lobby. Josh bought two grilled cheese sandwiches, which turned out to be depressingly black and hard and soaked in grease. At least he had something to fill his belly, he thought, remembering poor Mr. Dantell, the patient with the colon blockage. Josh counted his lucky stars for the privilege of being able to eat and digest semi-edible sandwiches.

He returned to his room to eat and catch up on his journal reading. Half-way through a boring article on liver cancer research, Josh put down his journal and thought about his day. Thornton's system, as brutal as it was, seemed to work. Of course, the lower-level staff members—the coolies, Nelson called them—appeared to do the brunt of the work, and Josh was sure they suffered because of it. However, there was "law and order," efficiency and civilization. He had always longed for those things when he was in the army, where every day was hectic and no one truly seemed to care about the health of the patients.

He fell asleep around ten o'clock but was up several times throughout the night, checking on the patients in the ward. He awoke around five thirty to begin the day, and after a quick breakfast of orange juice and a Danish, he entered the ward. Nelson had just started rounds when Josh joined the group. Their first stop was at Mr. Dantell's room, to wish him good luck.

When Josh completed his rounds, he found out he had been assigned a small locker and went there immediately. It was just a cubbyhole, barely larger than a breadbox. In it he found a green scrub suit and took it with him as he rushed to the pre-op room. The crew had just wheeled in Dantell and had him lined up with five other patients awaiting surgery that morning.

Josh walked up to Dantell, and again thought of his father. Dantell wasn't quite as old, but his eyes were just as full of fear and pain. Only the pain of cancer was as agonizing as the pain of a blocked colon, Josh thought, and he wished effective drugs were available to completely eradicate Dantell's torture. Whatever he was using was merely notching down the degree of pain, not stopping it.

He gently clasped the man's hand. "Mr. Dantell, it's Doctor Walker. You're in good hands. Try not to be nervous."

The man looked up at Josh through reddened eyes. "Doctor, I'm so cold." Dantell shivered as he fidgeted with the blanket that covered him. "I'm freezing. Can't you do something?" he whispered. His voice sounded as thin as dry as the feel of his skin.

"Your medication makes you feel cold," Josh said, "but I'll try to help." He turned to the nearest orderly. "Get Mr. Dantell another blanket, please." The fellow hesitated and started to say something, but Josh raised his voice and spoke again. "Another blanket. Now."

He turned back to his patient and sought some way to distract him from his pain and cold. "Mr. Dantell, when I was a little kid I had a blanket named Donny that I took everywhere. I wouldn't go to sleep without it, and I wouldn't trust anyone with it but my dad." Dantell nodded; maybe his own child had had such a comforting object.

When the orderly brought a blue acrylic blanket, Josh spread it out over Dantell and tucked it around him. "When you hold this blanket, Mr. Dantell," said Josh, "think of me. Imagine that I'm holding your hand. I'll be right beside you."

Dantell smiled, clenching and unclenching the blanket in his hands. The gesture worried Josh; he had seen too many people fidget with their blankets just before their deaths.

Suddenly Dantell sat bolt upright and stared into Josh's face with such intensity that Josh almost backed away. Instead he stood his ground and gripped Dantell's hand. Dantell squeezed back with incredible strength, but Josh ignored the pain. "Dr. Walker, I'm so afraid," Dantell rasped. "I'm so very afraid. I've got a beautiful wife, Doc, a wonderful woman. I don't...I don't want to leave her."

Josh patted Dantell on the shoulder, moved by the patient's fear. He had seen the same look so clearly before in his father's face, at the end. But this was different. This man would live.

"Don't be frightened, Mr. Dantell. Dr. Nelson is a superb surgeon.

You'll see your wife in the recovery room, and after a few days you'll be able to go home. Now relax. Everything is going to be okay. Hold on to your blanket, and remember that it's just the same as my hand."

Dantell let go of Josh's hand, clutched his blanket and gave Josh a small smile. While he didn't actually relax, he seemed at least resigned.

A short time later, the crew wheeled Dantell into the operating room and positioned him on the table. Josh watched as a nurse inserted IVs into the patient's arm and the anesthesia resident began infusing pentothal. Josh had heard that the anesthesia department was under the direct control of Thornton, who appropriated whatever monies the department could generate to the surgery department. This, Nelson had said, didn't do much to increase the chief's popularity.

Maybe this explained the anesthesia resident's angry expression, thought Josh, as the man looked up at Josh and scowled. "Who are you? Another greenie from the surgery department?"

Before he could answer, Dantell tried to roll over, and it was all Josh, the intern and the circulation nurse could do to hold him down. Finally Dantell went under, and after some fumbling with the endotracheal tube, the resident completed intubation.

For the first time, Josh began to feel the depth of Dantell's fear. Was he struggling against the anesthesia because he realized, on some level, that he might never come out of it?

Josh shook the notion from his head as he scrubbed and began prepping Dantell's abdomen. The scrub nurse came up to him and greeted him in a subdued voice. "You're Dr. Walker, aren't you? I'm Nancy Gallo."

Josh looked up for a moment and nodded. "Pleased to meet you." The nurse had wise brown eyes that reminded Josh of his favorite English teacher in junior high.

"Dr. Walker, the chart shows that this patient did not have a good bowel prep. Are you aware of that?"

Josh continued to wipe iodine on Dantell's distended belly as he mulled over an answer. "Well, Dr. Nelson told me last night that the patient was obstructed and they had done the best they could."

The nurse's gentle manner dissolved in a flare of muted anger. "Shit! Leave it to the residents to bring the patient up here in a half-assed condition! Let me tell you, if this was one of Thornton's private patients and he found out about these shenanigans, all your asses would be grass."

The Long Silk Line

Josh started, taken aback by her outburst. Not knowing what to say, or even if he should say anything, he finished prepping Dantell, then outlined the surgical field with green towels. Finally, he laid linen drapes over the whole matrix. After a few minutes that crawled by like hours, Josh saw Nelson come in, followed by Dr. Ravis. Josh knew that the chief surgical resident would not be permitted to perform major surgery without the assistance of an attending doctor.

For a moment, Josh stood in awe of the two men. They looked more like gods than humans, their posture perfect, their faces glowing with pride and intelligence. Nelson especially seemed like a doctor from an old TV show, his hair carefully groomed and not a thread out of place on him. It made Josh feel proud just to be in the company of such glittering professionals.

Josh watched as Nelson and Ravis scrubbed and gowned, and Nelson approached the right side of the patient. Ravis stood opposite him, watching Nelson's every move like a panther eyeing a rabbit. Nelson coughed and moved about restlessly, catching Josh off guard. Was Nelson nervous? He had seemed so confident and self-possessed just moments earlier. What was going on? thought Josh.

"What type of incision do you plan to make?" Ravis asked, as if he were issuing a challenge. Based on the sound of his voice, Josh thought that whatever Nelson would say, Ravis would say it was incorrect.

"Maybe a midline," Nelson sputtered. "I think that will give us good exposure." Nelson stared at the surgical field, obviously avoiding Ravis's cold stare.

"Don't use the word `us.' It's your exposure, man, so get to it."

At first Josh didn't understand what Ravis had said; his thick accent was hard to follow. When he did understand, Josh thought the surgeon was joking.

As Nelson ran a scalpel over the iodined skin, dark, bluish blood began to pour from the incision. "The blood's dark,"

Ravis snapped at the anesthesia resident, then sneered at Nelson. "Now what, boy?" This was no joke, thought Josh. Whatever Ravis was doing, he was most definitely serious about it.

"The blood's dark," Nelson repeated, and the anesthesiologist shook himself; it seemed to Josh that the man was rousing himself from a daydream.

The anesthesia dosage was adjusted, and after what seemed like hours to Josh, the team entered the abdominal cavity. Josh winced as he looked at the swollen, inflamed bowel. "My God!" Ravis gasped. "Couldn't you people get a bowel prep on this patient?"

"No, sir," said Nelson. "The patient has been obstructed and we just couldn't get the bowel to evacuate."

"Well, Dr. Nelson, this is going to be quite a struggle. It looks as if the colon, tumor and all, is fixed up against the ribcage and liver."

Josh studied Dantell, then looked at Nelson. His face was red and glistening with sweat. "I think we can do it if we mobilize the colon from the right side, sir," Nelson said, sliding his hand under the colon. Josh could see that Nelson's arm was trembling slightly.

"See here, Nelson," Ravis growled, "don't say `we,'. This is your case, but I think you should mobilize the colon from the left."

Nelson tugged strenuously on the swollen, right-hand portion of the bowel. Josh winced inside as the surgeon manhandled the distended tissue; the god-like surgeon was gone, replaced by a fumbling child.

The fluid within the lumen began to vibrate and shine like a watermelon under water, and Josh thought he saw a slight protrusion in the membrane. "Dr. Nelson, Dr. Ravis—look here." He pointed to the spot in question. "Could be diverticulitis...."

Josh stopped, noticing that the room was completely silent. Everyone was looking at him. "No one is interested in your opinion, doctor," Ravis said. "Just keep quiet and assist."

Josh hesitated. He knew the doctors might view him as arrogant and threatening, but he just couldn't remain silent while Dantell's life was at stake. Again he pointed to the small white spot on the man's bowel. "But look...."

Almost before he knew what was happening, Josh saw the bowel darken at the protrusion. A thin stream of fecal matter squirted from a tiny hole. He looked up to see Dr. Ravis shrink back, tugging on the left side of the colon. The bowel burst, causing a large rent in the liver. Blood and feces spewed over the entire surgical field.

Josh gasped as fecal matter struck his mask and forehead. Without thinking he raised his hand and tried to wipe his face.

"God! Sponges, quick! Stop the bleeding!" Ravis shouted, as the staff began packing the liver bed with lap pads.

"Good Lord, Dr. Walker has contaminated himself!" shouted Nancy Gallo. "He'll need a change of gloves." Josh shook his head as he continued to scrape the muck from his mask. A hideous odor filled his nostrils, and he had trouble breathing. From the corner of his eye he saw a nurse rush to the restroom and heard the sound of her retching.

"Damn it, man!" Ravis screamed at Nelson. "Get the bleeding under control or you—I mean *you*, not we—*you* will lose *your* patient."

Nelson seemed to rouse himself from a trance. Josh rescrubbed and regloved, and in fifteen minutes, Dantell's abdominal cavity was evacuated. Nevertheless, a milieu of blood and feces, and the nauseating smell, still remained. "Get the sucker and saline and clean out the belly, Dr. Walker, while we stop the bleeding," Ravis shouted. "Better get some blood, boy," he barked at Nelson. "This patient's going to need it."

Two hours later, Dantell was taken to intensive care and Josh took his first deep breath since the operation had begun. Ravis and Nelson had performed a colostomy and the wound was packed, but Dantell's blood pressure was low and there was no urine output. Josh hoped Dantell would make it.

As he entered the room to check on his patient, he saw Dantell's wife; it had to be her. A plump, friendly-looking woman with beautiful long black hair, she sat beside her husband, holding his limp hand and talking to him, though he was completely unconscious. It was a good thing, too, Josh thought, walking up to Mrs. Dantell and introducing himself. The man would feel nothing, unlike Josh's father, who had spent the last hours of his life wide awake, in horrifying agony.

"Thank you for all your help, doctor," Mrs. Dantell said. Her eyes were red, but she wasn't crying. Perhaps she had accepted her husband's death and mourned for him already.

If only she'd cry, Josh thought. Then he might be able to accept Dantell's impending death better himself. "I'm afraid I didn't do much," he mumbled, hoping he had cleaned his face thoroughly. "I sure wish I could have done more."

Her huge, luminous eyes reminded Josh of another man's wife, years ago, while he had been an intern in an army hospital. He had been assisting a doctor with a stress test on an older petty officer, when the man collapsed on the treadmill and died. A massive heart attack. Nothing could have saved him, and nothing did, though Josh, the doctor and the entire nursing staff did their best.

It was the first time he had ever seen an apparently healthy man die so suddenly, and the incident left him feeling hollow for days. He had dreaded telling the man's wife, and yet he'd had to; she hadn't wept either. It was Josh who had been next to tears as he walked the widow from department to department, going over information, filling out forms and getting clearances. It had been an excruciatingly sad experience, and he never wanted to have to do that again.

He tried to speak to Mrs. Dantell, to express his sorrow for her husband's condition, but he was just too overcome with fatigue and misery to say very much. After a few minutes, Josh briefly checked Dantell, whose vital signs, while stable, were skating on the edge of crisis, and excused himself. He headed for the doctor's lounge, nearly tripping over his own feet. "What a comedy of errors!" he overheard one doctor tell another on the way out of the lounge, and he knew at once that they were speaking of the botched surgery. Josh trudged into the quiet room and poured himself a cup of coffee.

He was trying to decide who was more to blame, Ravis or Nelson, when Nelson himself came up to him and laid his hand on Josh's back. "Dr. Walker, you look awful! When was the last time you got any sleep? Guess what? You did hear about the nursing shortage, didn't you? Well, you've been selected to stay with Mr. Dantell for the next 24 hours. You know—monitor his vital signs and give him medication, fluids. It'll be fun."

Josh shrugged off Nelson's hand. After what he'd witnessed in the operating room, he was in no mood for the chief resident's cruel jokes. "At least someone will be taking care of him," he mumbled, forcing his way past the resident.

"Hey! Don't let this stuff get to you!" Nelson called to him, but Josh ignored him.

Back at Dantell's bedside, Josh examined the man thoroughly. As pale and feeble as Dantell looked, Josh was surprised to find him still alive. Josh drew a blood count and sent it to the lab: Since the report came back showing a hemoglobin of eight, Josh ordered another two units of blood. Over the next few hours, despite all his efforts, Dantell's blood pressure continued to fall.

Josh collapsed in a chair by the bedside, holding his head in his hands. Dantell was dying, and the inevitability of his death was tearing Josh apart. He blamed himself for not standing up to two asinine doctors who couldn't agree on how to mobilize a colon. He thought of Dantell's wife again and could almost hear the surgeons overwhelming her with medical jargon and empty phrases in order to confuse her and cover their own incompetence. Doctors were divinities at St. Cahill's. They could do no wrong. "Unforeseeable complications arising from standard surgery"—that's what they'd say. Just one of those tragic things that happened now and then during major surgery. He knew what he would like to say to Mrs. Dantell, that two screw-ups had killed the man she loved through negligence and puerile bickering. But it would never be. He knew the truth, and he'd have to find a way to live with it or lose his job.

Josh had Nelson paged, and moments later the resident came to Dantell's room. "How's the patient?" he asked cheerily.

"Not so hot," Josh replied in a whisper, so as not to frighten Mrs. Dantell. Nelson never took a serious view of anything, even death. "Blood pressure 60 over 40 and not much urine output. I've done all I can, and frankly, I'm real worried for him. What do you suggest we do?"

Nelson craned his neck to look into the hall. "Is Nurse Dempsey here? The one with the cute butt?"

"Actually, she is, but I don't really see what...."

"Look, doctor, you've had a tough day," Nelson said, patting Josh's arm. "You're starved and exhausted. Why don't you take a breather? Go down and get something to eat while I take over, okay? Don't worry. Everything'll be fine."

Josh flinched, remembering that he had said the same thing to Dantell just before that fiasco of an operation. But he had eaten nothing since breakfast, and he reasoned that Nelson was right, that he really couldn't be of much help to Dantell if he was weak and sleepy from hunger. "Well, all right. Thanks. That would help me out. I won't be long. How about Mrs. Dantell? She's been here for hours. She could probably use a break, too."

"I sent her out for a while," Nelson said, smiling. "Poor woman looks haggard, doesn't she? Just like you. Go ahead, take your time." He looked positively happy, an odd emotional state, given the condition of his patient, but Josh quickly dismissed the troubling thought as he hurried to the cafeteria and the delightful fragrance of roast beef, fresh rolls and hot apple pie struck him in the nose. Josh passed Ravis at the door and said hello to him, but the short Swede merely frowned and grunted; that was as much acknowledgement as Ravis was prepared to give a new resident, and Josh was pleased to have gotten even such short shrift. Most surgeons ignored residents altogether.

Josh bought a chicken dinner with mashed potatoes and butterscotch pudding. As he found a place to sit, he caught a glimpse of Mrs. Dantell buying a cup of coffee and a piece of blueberry pie. He waved to her, but she didn't see him; the poor woman was dead on her feet, he thought, dreading the sorrow that the next few hours would surely bring.

Josh was just diving into his potatoes when he overheard bits of conversation from the nurses at the next table. They were talking about Dantell's disastrous operation.

"...awful. Shit everywhere."

"...all over the floor...."

"...he and Ravis tore the bowel wide open...."

"...jerks...."

"...expect that of Nelson, wouldn't you?"

"...doesn't give a damn about anyone but himself. Thinks he's God's gift...."

"...God's goof-up is more like it. Poor Mr. Dantell!"

Josh wolfed down his food and drowned it with a glass of milk. Though he felt exhausted, he knew he had to get back to the ICU as soon as possible. Nelson's generous gesture now seemed highly suspect. If the nurses didn't trust him, why should anyone else?

He looked around for Mrs. Dantell, but she was gone.

When he returned to Dantell's room, Nelson was nowhere in sight. "Goddamn bastard!" Josh said, calling for a nurse. Dantell was struggling for air. Josh immediately took the man's blood pressure.

A nurse rushed into the room. "Dr. Walker!" she gasped. "Mr. Dantell! My God! What's wrong?"

"Blood pressure is 40!" Josh shouted, trying to clear Dantell's airway. "He can't breathe. Quick! Get the staff in here on the double. Find Nelson. Alert Ravis. Willowby's in the cafeteria. Get him here too."

In a moment the room was filled with doctors, nurses and interns, all trying to resuscitate the failing patient. Josh reached for the Ambu bag to try to help him but Dantell was aspirating. Ravis raced up to Josh and began working on the patient, trying to revive him. Josh grabbed one nurse by the arm. "Where's Nelson?"

She gave him a pained look and shook her head. "Look, I don't want to cause any trouble...."

"Damn it! There's plenty of trouble already!" he exploded. "Where he is?"

The nurse, who couldn't have been more than twenty, nodded, her gaze fixed on the floor. "Try the staff restroom right behind the nurses' lounge," she said at last. "Only don't say that I told you anything."

Dazed and angry, Josh pushed his way through the confusion of hospital staff and made his way to the nurses's lounge. A light was on in the restroom, and he flung open the door. There was Nelson, sitting on a toilet in one of the cubicles. A slender nurse, stark naked, was straddling his lap, fulled engaged in the rhythms of passion. Wet noises filled the stall. "Get out of here, Walker!" Nelson panted. The nurse continued her gyrations, and Nelson's face began to glow with ecstacy.

"Like shit I will!" Josh flung himself into the stall, pushed aside the nurse and grabbed Nelson by the collar, hauling him up off the toilet seat. "You fucking bastard! A man's dying because you couldn't wait 15 minutes for a screw! Get the hell back to ICU before I break your neck!"

Nelson was a muscular man, but Josh was empowered by the strength of rage. He dragged Nelson out of the stall, the surgeon zipping up his pants as he stumbled forward, then jogged down the hall, cursing. Josh looked around for the nurse; she had vanished.

It was already too late. The staff was still working over Dantell, but Ravis was shaking his head. Josh walked up to the man's lifeless body and picked up a pale hand. For a long time he sat holding that hand, pressing it against his face. He had told Dantell he'd be there for him, but he hadn't. Josh had all but deserted his patient. He should have known better than to trust a reptile like Nelson.

Slowly the nurses began filtering back to their positions. One told Josh that Mrs. Dantell had been taken to a waiting room and was expecting a doctor to escort her through the appropriate departments. "She's knows," the nurse whispered.

"I'll...I'll talk to her," Josh said to Ravis, who nodded and left the unit. "I can't believe this is happening," Josh groaned to himself, dreading the next hour. Just as he rose to leave, he looked up and saw Nelson standing beside him. The resident examined the body, then gave a huge sigh. "Well, well. What a shame. And I thought we did such a nice job, too."

Josh could barely repress his anger. He clenched his fist; he never wanted to hit someone as much as he wanted to punch Nelson that very moment. "Hell, man, you did a lousy job! And...and you abandoned the patient! I can't believe it! You over-sexed maniac!

Dr. Thornton was right to ban sex here." Somehow he managed to keep his voice to an outraged whisper. "You...you set me up so you could get a little action! You murderer!"

"Now, now," Nelson said, patting Josh's shoulder. "I didn't set anyone up, and I didn't mean to cause any trouble. Dempsey came in and one thing led to another. That's all." His face was still red from his conquest; he even smelled of sex. "I swear, I asked a nurse to cover for me. It's her fault, not mine."

Josh shook his head and began backing out of the room.

"You're not going to tell Thornton about this, are you?" Nelson murmured.

"Maybe I will," Josh said. "Whatever happens, you can be damn sure I'm not going to forget it. Now you'll have to excuse me...I have to talk to Mrs. Dantell." His heart hammered inside him as he turned and blundered his way toward the waiting room.

3

Josh approached Mrs. Dantell in the waiting room; they were alone, save for one other woman asleep on a couch. "Please stay seated," he began. "I'm sorry...."

"It's all right, doctor," she said, nodding sadly. "I could tell by the way you carried yourself." Josh took in her face, which appeared to collapse as she spoke, folding in on itself. She didn't cry. "I know he's dead." She sank into her chair, but she didn't make a sound, just like the other widow Josh had talked to years ago. She looked as if she had taken a bullet in the heart and was slowly dying. But she didn't cry.

If she had, Josh knew he would be all right, but he couldn't bear the sight of that destroyed woman. He reported the entire surgery and its aftermath to her—only because it was his duty, not that she was interested in the details—and helped her make the rounds of the various departments and fill out the legion of forms. But afterwards he didn't know what to say or do and stood staring at her dumbly, hoping he might yet come up with some comforting remark.

Mrs. Dantell took his hand, and finally gave vent to her tears. They streaked her cheeks as she tried to smile. "Thank you, doctor. You look exhausted. Can't you get some sleep now?"

Josh stared at her in amazement: Here she was, suddenly bereft of her husband, and it was *she* who was consoling *him*. Unable to think of a reply, he threw his arms around her and hugged her hard against his chest.

At that moment he knew what he had to do. Nelson would have to pay for this woman's pain.

It was early morning when Mrs. Dantell left. As soon as he could Josh went to Thornton's office and requested a meeting with chief in Nelson's presence. He'd get to the heart of the matter and make certain that Nelson was disciplined for his gross neglect. Hadn't Thornton himself warned the interns against becoming sexually involved with the staff? Thornton would blow his top.

Later that morning Josh was summoned to Thornton's office. He was ecstatic. When Josh arrived at Thornton's office, Nelson was already in the anteroom, tapping his long fingers against his lean legs. As Josh sat down opposite him, Nelson scowled but said nothing. The two spent fifteen minutes elaborately avoiding each other's gaze.

At last Eileen called them both inside to see the chief, and they sat down in leather chairs in front of Thornton's gleaming walnut desk. Thornton presided over his desk like a judge over his bench, his face stern and unreadable. He looked at Josh, then Nelson. "Dr. Nelson, Dr. Walker has made me aware of this...this incident involving Mr. Dantell. You know there are strict rules concerning sexual activity among staff members, and I expect you, as well as everyone else, to obey those rules. Is that understood?"

"Yes, sir," Nelson said in a chastened voice. He hung his head like a repentant child.

"Very good. Thank you, Dr. Nelson. You may leave now."

Josh watched in shock as Nelson walked slowly out the door, the picture of humility. That's all he was going to get? A rap on the fingers? At St. Vincent's Academy, where Josh had gone to grade school, he had been punished far worse for talking in class.

"Dr. Walker," Thornton continued, turning to Josh. Josh leaned forward, unsure what to expect. Thornton was scowling, and his face was as dark as a thundercloud. "I cannot and will not tolerate...snitching from my professional staff. The affront you did to Dr. Nelson was unforgivable and, under other circumstances, could even have damaged his reputation. Telling tales out of school is unconscionable, and I will not, I repeat, not allow it."

As Thornton paused to take a breath, Josh rallied his wits and tried to understand what was going on. Thornton was berating *him* for exposing Nelson's outrageous behavior? He could scarcely believe it. "But sir, consider the consequences. Because of Dr. Nelson's actions, Mr. Dantell was left unattended for some time. Had we gotten to him earlier...."

Thornton's eyebrows rose in a gesture of triumph. "And just who was responsible for staying with the patient, Dr. Walker? It was not Dr. Nelson's duty at the time, I believe."

"I plead guilty to trusting Dr. Nelson," Josh persisted, "but...."

"I'm not finished! Please don't interrupt!" growled Thornton. "You're in enough hot water as it is, Dr. Walker, and if it happens again, you'll have only yourself to blame for the consequences. Did Dr. Nelson commit a breach of hospital rules? No question of that. But there are proper ways of dealing with these infractions, doctor, and you *will* learn these ways. If you confront an issue like this head on again, I will have to take disciplinary actions."

This was sheer lunacy, thought Josh. Nelson abandoned a patient, and he got a mild reprimand. He, Josh, exposed the egregious error, and he got lambasted. And just what other "ways" were there of revealing and punishing incompetence? Again he tried to speak for himself. "Doctor Thornton, I...."

"Dr. Walker, because you're new here, I'm going to be lenient with you," Thornton answered, ignoring him. "Consider yourself warned. Return to your work and remember...I don't want to have any more of this unprofessional behavior from you."

Josh staggered out the office, his head spinning with hurt and confusion. When he reached the hallway, he saw Nelson waiting for him, leaning against the wall as if he had nothing better to do.

"Look at your face, doctor," he said. "Cardiac trouble? Or maybe just premature ejaculation." Nelson clapped him on the back, but Josh shrugged away from him. He hated the feel of Nelson's hand.

"What did Daddy say, Joshie? Did Daddy frighten little Joshie?" Nelson's huge grin lit up his face.

"Go to hell," Josh grumbled.

"Aw, Josh is upset. Don't let Daddy rattle you, Dr. Walker. As you may have guessed, the old man's sort of fond to me."

"I've...I've never seen such blatant favoritism in my life," Josh hissed under his breath. "It's sick."

"Jealous, are we?" Nelson leaned close, and Josh pulled away. "All joshing aside, Josh, I strongly urge you to stay out of my face and my business. Got it?"

"Believe me, Dr. Nelson, I want to have as little to do with you as possible," Josh said. He turned away and hurried down the hall, his throat aching with rage.

That night, Josh dragged himself up to his room, all energy sapped, and threw himself on his bed. Mrs. Dantell's shattered face haunted his mind.

This wasn't the way it was supposed to work out. How had Nelson managed to fool Thornton? Or did Thornton know something that Josh didn't? In any case, the result had been the same: Dr. Nelson had license to do as he pleased, even at the expense of the patients.

He heard a knock at his door. It was Willowby. "Dr. Walker, I heard about Dantell. I couldn't come to help; I had to assist in emergency. Sorry."

Josh mumbled something, but he wasn't sure what he was saying.

"What?" said Willowby. "For Christ's sake, man, speak up."

"I said, did you know what happened?" Josh said.

Willowby nodded. "Nurse Dempsey told me. She was screwing Nelson when Nelson was supposed to be monitoring Mr. Dantell. Dantell went into crisis, and that was that."

Josh covered his eyes with his arm, trying to block out the obscene truth of the intern's assessment. "Does that seem right to you?"

Willowby came in and sat down beside him. "Of course not. But then, 'right' isn't what St. Cahill's does best. That goddamn Nelson! One of these days he's going to do something so stupid and ugly that I'm going to have to report him."

Josh bolted upright in his bed. "What? What could be more stupid and ugly than causing a patient to die because you're too horny to attend to him?" Was Willowby crazy? Was the entire hospital crazy? Or was he?

Willowby placed his hand on Josh's knee. "Listen, I know it sounds nuts, but that's the way things operate around here, so to speak. Nobody tells on anybody, and we cover each others' butts. What happened today was the exception...really. A fluke. I mean, we make mistakes, but hardly anyone ever dies because of it. You do know that Nelson is Thornton's fair-haired boy, don't you? He can do no wrong. How could Thornton's personal protege make a mistake? It's unthinkable. Nelson could set fire to the hospital, and Thornton would find some excuse for him. I hope you're not planning anything stupid, like trying to snitch on him. Thornton would have you hustled out of here faster than Grant took Richmond."

"Not quite that fast," Josh muttered.

"What?" Willowby's cheeks puffed out as round and red as two ripe apples. "What do you mean?"

Josh swung his feet over the side of the bed and stood up. "I mean that your kind advice is too late. I've already spoken to Thornton." Josh gave Willowby a quick account of the disastrous meeting.

"Can't say I'm surprised he screwed you and not Nelson." Willowby paused to light a cigarette. "But I'm shocked that you survived. Jeez! You're lucky! Keep your mouth shut from now on, okay? Trust me, you don't want to blow this opportunity. Finish your training here and your future is made. You'll be golden. Then you can act like Dr. Kildare if you want." Willowby exhaled a cloud of smoke into the center of the room. "Up until then, silence is golden."

Josh coughed. He hated the smell of cigarette smoke, but Willowby had come to him in kindness and friendship, and Josh didn't want to alienate him. "You know, maybe I'm not cut out for this sort of thing—the in-fighting, the politics. I can't believe there are so many personal problems among the staff."

Willowby nodded. "Hey, you put together so many strong-willed, egotistic people in one place and the sparks are bound to fly. I know you feel bad about Dantell, but try to forget it. What happened today was awful, I'll give you that. But it was a fluke. You know as well as yourself that anything can happen once you open up someone's abdomen. It was just in the cards for this guy, that's all."

"Maybe," Josh conceded, though the incident still troubled him deeply. Was Willowby right? Maybe he had to get past Dantell's death, let it go. Patients died every day. Hell, surgeons were in the business of life and death. Maybe it really was just a tragic mishap. If so, he certainly had no business judging who, if anyone, should be blamed.

This all sounded sensible enough, but somehow he just couldn't convince himself. Right was right, he thought, and wrong was intolerable.

"Here, take this." Willowby pressed a soft, warm package into Josh's hand. It was a packet of Hostess chocolate cupcakes. "Good for the soul."

But not for the heart, thought Josh. He accepted the cakes anyway. "Thanks, Willowby."

Willowby started to leave, then turned at the doorway and smiled at Josh. "Say, I almost forgot! Guess what I heard?"

Josh shook his head. "Let's see...I've been designated as the new Surgeon General?"

"Good guess. But wrong. I heard the chief talking about

you this afternoon. Seems they're going to kick you upstairs to Jack Radcliff's lab. He runs a think tank on the fourth floor and designs artificial heart valves for Dr. God."

"Why do they want me to work with him?" Josh wondered aloud.

"Hey, man, this is a promotion. Be happy!"

"Promotion?" Josh sat back down on his bed in confusion. This was just the chance he had been looking for, an opportunity to work on experimental medicine, become a pioneer. But why now?

"I don't get it. Why a promotion? A few hours ago, Thornton was about to chew my head off."

Willowby took the package of cupcakes from Josh, broke it open and contemplated his smudged fingers. "Well, you do need to get started on a research project as soon a possible. Thornton wasn't kidding when he said you're expected to produce papers, and Radcliff's in charge of all the research projects."

"Yes," Josh said, "or it could be Thornton's way of keeping me out of trouble."

Willowby nodded. "If you really want to get nasty, then you might even suspect that Thornton was trying to bribe you to be quiet...you know, things'll go fine for you if you keep your nose out of other people's shit."

A feeling of hopelessness rose in Josh's heart. "It couldn't be that," he whispered. He wouldn't let himself believe that his good fortune was nothing more than blackmail.

"Naw, probably not." Willowby handed Josh a slightly crushed cupcake, then bit into the other. Around a mouthful of crumbs managed to say, "Congratulations! Here's to you, Dr. Halstead."

They solemnly toasted each other with the gooey cakes. "I'm glad you're not leaving," Willowby said, his mouth full. "Now for God's sake, keep your trap shut and mind your own business. Otherwise, you're out of here." He stretched out his sticky hand toward Josh. "Good luck, Dr. Walker. You're going to need it."

Josh smiled wryly and shook hands. "Better wash up before you go on call," he said. "There's enough dirt around here as it is."

4

Josh BEGAN TO put Dantell's death behind him. He couldn't believe it was a fluke, as Willowby had said, just a tragic accident; it had been a mistake, but he couldn't afford to dwell on other people's mistakes. He found with the passing of the days that he didn't think about it often, as long as he confined his relationship with Nelson to a professional level. No lunches together, no "favors," no chit-chat. Now that he knew Nelson's special position and how he took advantage of it, such avoidance suited Josh fine.

During his rounds and in the operating room, he tried to help his patients all he could, comforting them as well as trying to heal them. He answered their questions, brought them information when they requested it, and sometimes simply held their hands.

It wasn't easy, considering he knew he averaged only five hours of sleep a day, but he was proud to think that all this hardship was helping his patients.

As Willowby had predicted, Josh was sent to Radcliff's lab one beautiful Monday morning, just after Josh had witnessed a spectacular red and orange sunrise from his tiny twelfth-floor window. He took it as a good omen.

Josh had done some research himself on Dr. Radcliff. The man had a glowing reputation throughout the local medical scene as a promising experimenter and a brilliant scholar. He had done his general surgical training at a respected West Coast training center, and had just completed his cardiovascular training under Thornton. In charge of the cardiovascular lab and all heart surgery at St.Cahill's, Radcliff had developed an artificial heart valve for the chief, called the Thornton Valve. Josh knew that clinical trials on several patients had just begun, and he was excited as he made his way to the research lab. This was the work he wanted to see and participate in; this was the work he saw as the most important aspect of his training.

Radcliff welcomed Josh to the lab with a grin and a friendly slap on the back. He was a tall, slender man with thinning black hair and bright brown eyes. "Welcome to my laboratory, my boy," he said, in a fair impression of Boris Karloff. He and an assistant led Josh on a tour around the lab, and Josh fairly leaped out of his skin with eagerness. "This is perfect," Josh blurted, running his hand over one of Radcliff's prototype heart monitors.

He loved this place already. He didn't need to be working with losers like Nelson; he could be a pioneer of medical technology.

"Yes, you can forget rounds," Radcliff said. "Here's where a doctor can really contribute to medicine and put himself squarely on the cutting edge of technology. The true advances in medical science are made in places just like this. And you can be a part of it, doctor, if you play your cards right."

"I was just thinking the same thing," Josh replied. He was surprised how quickly he was willing to play whatever game Radcliff wanted.

"Look at this little beauty," Radcliff said, holding up a small metal box containing a life-like, metal-and-plastic heart valve. "You won't find anything like this anywhere in the world," he said, not even trying to disguise the sound of pride in his voice. "We had a dozen made up at the foundry. God, they're damned expensive! But worth it."

Josh examined the small mechanical device, held up by wires in a clear plastic enclosure within the metal box. He felt awed, as if Radcliff had handed him some precious relic.

After a few moments, Josh realized that something was missing. He should have been able to hear the faint barking of dogs from the doctor's dog lab, but the place was perfectly silent. "Dr. Radcliff, I'd really like to see your dog lab, if I may," he said reverently.

"We don't have a dog lab, Dr. Walker."

"You mean you test out this device using dogs from other facilities?" asked Josh, intrigued.

Radcliff shook his head. "No, I mean that we don't use dogs for testing at all. Believe me, I've gone over these devices intensively. I am one hundred percent assured of their performance before I place them in a patient."

Josh gazed at the doctor, temporarily at a loss of words. A man like Radcliff had to know what he was doing, but to not test the devices on dogs first....Did Radcliff have some alternative testing procedure that he was loath to reveal? "Isn't that a bit irregular?" Josh asked, then hurriedly added, "but just the sort of bold move an innovative scientist should make." Radcliff swelled with pride until he looked like a blowfish about to explode.

Suddenly Josh recalled an idea that he hoped Radcliff might appreciate. "You know, sir, I was reading in one of the journals about a mechanical system that can be set up in a lab— a pulse duplicator system—to test valves before insertion. You can measure pressures and even see the flow patterns. It's fantastic. There's even talk of someday being able to computerize mathematical models of the system, the blood flow and...."

Radcliff broke in, and Josh's words trailed off. "I've looked into that research," he said with a contemptuous flick of his hand. "It's value has been highly over-rated. Don't believe all you read, doctor. Trust me, after the preliminary design and testing, hands-on experimentation with the patients themselves is the only way to go in this field. Most of the patients we consider are virtually dying, anyway. This valve will be like a new lease on life for them, a miracle."

Josh studied the valve again. A trace of skepticism about Radcliff's boastful claims crept into his mind. The harder he tried to push it away, the stronger it nagged at him. "How many have you implanted?" he asked.

"Only two. However, I am performing the third implant

tomorrow morning—Mr. McDermot on 5B, medical with a mitral problem. Come to the O.R. at 7:30 and you'll see surgical history in the making."

"Sure. I'll be there with bells on." Josh left the lab in a daze. So much was happening so fast, and most of it contradicted his medical training. But then he had never been in the big leagues before. Maybe, he reasoned, geniuses just take more chances.

Either Radcliff was a genius or a madman. Time would tell. As he had found out in the military, sometimes there wasn't much difference between the two. The commanders who looked as if they had no compunction about throwing away their soldiers lives, at least in war games, were often the best strategists, the men who actually saved the most lives through brilliant deployment. Maybe Radcliff was such a man.

Josh immediately went to 5B to study McDermot's chart. As he entered the ward, he saw Sam Cantini, the cardiology resident, whom he had met the day before. "Hello, Dr. Walker," Cantini said in a pleasant voice. "Can I help you?"

"Well, yes, doctor," Josh said. "I wanted to see Mr. McDermot. You know, the patient that Radcliff is going to operate on tomorrow."

Suddenly Cantini's face turned bright red. He motioned for Josh to come with him, and as they stepped into the hallway, he erupted. "God, you butchers! You're all the same! Leave the poor man alone! Read my consultation on the chart." Cantini's voice trembled with contempt.

Josh took a step backward, bowled over by the cardiologist's hostility. "I'm sorry. I didn't mean to cause any trouble. Obviously I don't know the whole story. Care to enlighten me?"

"That Radcliff!" Cantini snarled in a deep voice. "Always looking for a piece of meat to butcher. Well, he can't have McDermot. The man's just too sick to undergo an operation, and he sure shouldn't be used as some kind of rat for Radcliff to experiment on. The poor guy's probably going to die any day, and he should just be allowed to cast off in peace, with some dignity."

"Of course," Josh said, rubbing his hands together as he fought to keep his composure. "But maybe Dr. Radcliff's valve can save his life. Isn't it a risk worth taking, if Mr. McDermot's prognosis is so grave?"

"No!" Cantini slapped his hand against the wall so hard that a passing nurse stopped and stared at him a moment before moving on. "Listen, McDermot has severe pulmonary hypertension," he continued in a lower tone. "Even if the operation were a success, which I personally doubt, he'd never survive the trauma. So forget it. That operation ain't gonna happen, and I'm going to see to it. Understand?"

"Yes...yes. Hey, to operate or not is *not* my call," murmured Josh. He felt terrible that Cantini, a friendly fellow with a quick wit, seemed to hold him in the same contempt he held Dr. Radcliff. "But you're mistaken if you think Dr. Radcliff or I want anything but what's best for the patient."

Cantini leaned forward and looked Josh right in the eye. "You think so, huh? You've got a lot to learn, doctor." Then he turned and walked briskly down the corridor.

That's the end of that. Cantini would get Radcliff to cancel the surgery, and the surgeon's new valve would have to wait for some other opportunity to prove its worth. He couldn't help but think of the pulse duplicator system. Surely the *New England Journal of Medicine* wouldn't have praised the technique so highly if it didn't have some merit. Josh's mind was whirling with questions and doubts as he dragged himself to his room.

The next morning at 7:00, as Josh began to make working rounds, the ward clerk called him. "Dr. Walker, it's Dr. Radcliff. He wants you immediately in O.R. Number 5."

"God! I thought they had canceled the case."

Josh rushed up to the operating room and donned a green scrub suit. As he entered the O.R., he found a large entourage of operating personnel in the "heart room," as they called the place.

Mr. McDermot, looking thin and frail, lay on the table, tubing extending from his nose and mouth; the pump team was ready to connect them to an oxygenator. Sitting majestically on the scrub nurses' Mayo stand was the Thornton Valve, in its shiny plastic container.

Josh nudged Radcliff as the researcher donned his scrub gown. "Dr. Radcliff, I went to the ward last night to see the patient, but the cardiology resident told me the operation was canceled."

"Oh, yeah?" Radcliff said with a wink. "Guess again."

"But his consultation," Josh began. "It said...."

"We tore up his consultation. He's only a goddamn resident, with lots to learn. We have to do what's right to save this patient's life. Right?" Josh nodded. "Now go scrub."

As Josh scrubbed his hands, his mind was torn between outrage and concern. Radcliff had a lot of gall to rebuff Cantini, but if he did so for the right reasons—to save McDermot's life—then how could he be wrong? Josh was still tortured by doubt as he entered the surgical field. The cardiac team had performed the median sternotomy, splitting the sternum and exposing the cardiac system. The patient had been hooked up to the pump and placed on bypass. Everything seemed to be going perfectly.

While Josh watched, Radcliff opened the left auricular appendage and exposed the mitral valve from above. The valve leaflets were fixed, and Radcliff excised the valve. Josh noticed that he myocardium limped along, as if it were a bystander watching the whole procedure, but not a vital part of it. Radcliff and his colleagues sewed the shiny metallic valve in place in minutes. The whole procedure had taken less than an hour. Josh sighed, impressed by the skill of the surgical team.

Radcliff closed the left auricle with meticulously neat sutures, then shouted to the pump team. "Off bypass. Let's see how it goes."

The team clamped the bypass lines, and the myocardium

came alive. But after a few moments the left auricular appendage began to swell like a balloon. "On bypass!" Radcliff yelled. "We have a problem. Got to open the auricular appendage again."

As Radcliff opened the chamber, Josh could see that the valve leaflets had fused with the blood and refused to budge. "Damn it!" Radcliff growled. "Do we have another sterile valve up here? This thing isn't working."

Josh froze. His own heart felt like a brick in his chest.

The scrub nurse shook her head. The team glanced at each other.

"What should we do, doctor?" a nurse cried out.

Josh stood in helpless anger, recalling what Cantini had said about Radcliff experimenting on McDermot like a rat. If the doctor had used animal hosts, the patient might not be in crisis right now.

After several frustrating minutes, Radcliff announced the only reasonable solution. "We have to transport him, pump and all, to Good Samaritan on the North Side. Dr. Roberts there is set up to handle just this sort of emergency. Get him on the phone immediately."

Josh watched the team prepare McDermot for his journey and load him onto elevator on the way to the ambulance. In a way, Josh wanted to go with the man, to watch this even play out, but he couldn't do it. The patient was all but dead; nothing could save him now, and there was no point in trying to reassure an unconscious man. Josh wished he could wash his hands of this butchery.

As the team was taking McDermot from the elevator, a hose pump burst. Josh and the team did what they could, but the man died on the stretcher, halfway between the elevator and the hall. Josh returned to his room exhausted; Cantini was standing by the door.

"I heard about McDermot," he said in a toneless voice.

"Sam, I'm sorry..." Josh began. He didn't get far.

"Yeah, sorry, that's going to help McDermot all right. Did you know that man had five kids? Irish Catholic, devout Christian. Went to church each Sunday. And you guys couldn't even let him die a decent death! You had to cut him to pieces first!"

"Listen, it wasn't like that at all!" Josh protested.

"Oh? Then how was it like?" sneered Cantini.

Josh paused. How had it been? For a while, the operation had seemed like the right thing to do, even in failure. "Radcliff was magnificent. His technique was flawless. Evidently that one pump had developed a flaw."

"Oh, spare me!" Cantini shouted.

"Calm down and listen to me!" Josh shouted, warming to his rationalization. "Radcliff had checked it out thoroughly, but...well, who knows what happened? Artificial heart components are still in the experimental stages, after all."

"That's my pointt exactly!" raged Cantini, banging his fist so loudly on Josh's door that the wood shook. "Radcliff was using McDermot as a guinea pig!"

"No, it wasn't that way!" cried Josh, clutching Cantini by the shoulders. "Listen! McDermot died, but it was a noble death. Just think how much Radcliff and the team learned in that operation. Using that information, they might be able to save the next patient. There is no other way for medicine to advance." Josh rubbed his sleeve across his sweating forehead. He sounded just like Radcliff. What was he doing?

Cantini closed his eyes, then opened them, and Josh could see he was making a tremendous effort to calm himself down. "Using my patients as so much experimental flesh does not strike me as noble," he said slowly, his voice shaking. "Look, I know you're idealistic. You like to think the best of people and you trust in technology to save lives. That's fine. But don't let yourself be blinded by the light, Walker. This isn't Disney World, and you're not Peter Pan. It's time to grow up."

The cardiologist shook himself free from Josh's grasp and trudged down the hall toward the elevators. Josh leaned against the door, feeling all his remaining strength drain from his body. During the operation, he had doubted Radcliff almost as much as Cantini did; so why did he take Radcliff's side against Cantini? Maybe it was because he really believed the valve would work and save lives, with a few modifications. Or maybe it was because he wanted so desperately for that valve to work, to be part of its development.

The questions were too much to contend with; he was exhausted. He had to sleep. It was all he could do to drag himself into his sweltering room, remove his clothes and flop down in his bed, hoping for a breeze.

Summer gradually worked its way into autumn. The weather grew cooler, the leaves on trees in the parks and on the sidewalks changed from green to rust and yellow, and everywhere Josh smelled the subtle scent of death and decay.

One evening, while he was eating dinner in the cafeteria, Josh realized he was becoming a little more weary every day. Days, nights, rounds, operating room schedules and post operative care all blurred together into one aching, demanding reality. There was no relief. He'd had to be careful not to burn himself out.

As he was running over his schedule and wondering how he was going to make it through the next week alive, Sperling Nelson came up and sat down next to him. "What's up, doctor?" Nelson asked, his face glowing with a white grin.

"Nothing," Josh said, looking down into his plate of meatloaf and green beans. He didn't have anything to say to Nelson; ever since the fiasco with Dantell, he had no trust in the man whatsoever.

"Hey, I know you've been avoiding me," Nelson said softly, his grin fading. "Still sore about me and Dempsey?"

Josh poked a piece of meatloaf around on his plate. He didn't want to speak with Nelson or re-open old wounds, but he didn't know how to respond with anything but the truth. "That man didn't have to die, doctor. Okay, I'm willing to believe that what happened on the table was an accident. Just one of those strokes of fate. But when you left the patient alone...and *why* you did it...."

"Come on," said Nelson. He stood up and grabbed Josh by the elbow. "I want to show you something."

"I'm not done eating," Josh objected, pulling his arm away.

Nelson laughed. "This is more important than food. Don't

worry. I'll buy you another dinner. Cross my heart, hope to undergo vascular surgery under Dr. Ravis."

Josh hesitated, then gave in. As much as he disliked Nelson, it was hard to stay permanently angry at him. Why try? "Okay, okay," he said, rising. He took a final gulp of milk. "What do you want to show me?"

Nelson led the way to the top of the roof, where two giant exhaust fans made a tremendous racket. Night was just beginning to fall, and the lights were coming on all over the city. To Josh, it looked like a peaceful twilight fairyland, even though the fans hurt his ears with their constant thunder.

"See that big building, the one with the blue lights?" Nelson said, pointing out a giant black monolith in the distance.

"Sure. That's the LakeCorps Building," Josh shouted.

"Wasn't there a big hullabaloo when it went up—something about some construction workers being killed and the company being negligent."

"Yeah, I guess. But it sure is commanding, isn't it? Just like Dr. "God" Thornton."

Josh looked at Nelson in disgust. "What's your point?" he shouted. These fans are killing me. Why did you bring me up here?"

"Do you know what they do?" yelled Nelson.

"What? The fans?"

Nelson laughed. "No, idiot, the folks at LakeCorps."

Josh thought for a moment, remembering an article he had read in the local paper months ago. "They're in machining, I believe. They make metal parts for airplane engines and the automotive industry, to be specific."

"Actually, not very specific, Dr. Walker. LakeCorps produces all the machined parts used in Radcliff's and Thornton's devices—like his specialized portal venal shunt equipment, the Thornton Valve, and his other big "invention," the Thornton Bracket.

"Yes, the calibrated frame for brain surgery," Josh said. The noise of the fans was really getting to him now, and he felt as if his skull were being fitted with a metal bracket. Without anesthesia. He held his hand to his forehead and pressed hard.

"So?"

"Well, Dr. Smartass," shouted Nelson, "Mr. Lake is chairman of the board at St. Cahill's. He's also the chairman of National Steel Corporation, Lake National Bank and Caribbean Oil."

Suddenly Josh understood. "A man like that must wield a lot of power. And he certainly has a lot of vested interest in Thornton and the hospital. I guess the chief treats him with kid gloves. But why tell me all this?"

To his surprise, Josh found himself being hustled off the roof and down to the twelfth floor. When he and Nelson reached Nelson's room, the chief resident spoke up. "Couldn't stand those fans anymore myself," he admitted. "Look here, Walker, you're smart. You've charmed the pants off a lot of people here, and don't get me wrong. I admire that. But I don't want to see you get yourself involved in something you can't handle. The rule around here is, `I didn't see it. I don't know what you're talking about.' Got it?"

Josh didn't know what to make of Nelson. Was he crazy? Or was he, in his own peculiar way, trying to help? Then a thought dawned on him. "Does this have anything to do with my suggestion to Dr. Radcliff about the computer modeling system I suggested for his valve?"

Nelson shrugged. "Radcliff doesn't like computer technology, mainly because Thornton doesn't like it. It's not part of the long silk line, you know. Besides, what if someone tried to calibrate that valve or the Portal caval shunt apparatus or the bracket using computer technology and discovered that all three of them were dead off-center?"

"But...but...that's exactly why you *should* use such a program," sputtered Josh. "If the devices aren't working properly, they should be tested."

"Yeah?" Nelson sneered. "Think so? And what if patients discover that those devices haven't been tested and calibrated 'properly,' to use your word. Can you see the lawsuits? Not just against St. Cahill's, but against LakeCorps, too. I suggest you forget about using much computerization around here, Dr. Walker. And if I were you I'd be mighty careful about what you say to people. When in doubt, keep your thoughts to yourself."

Josh gulped down a mouthful of bile. How he hated to be caught adrift this way, not knowing what was happening or how to react. "I'll be careful," he said, wondering just what he should be careful about. "You can be assured that I won't do anything to embarrass the hospital or to risk Mr. Lake's involvement on the board, if that's what you mean."

Nelson laughed and tapped Josh on the forehead. "Smart lad, Walker," he chuckled. "The less you know around here, the better, Walker. Just keep your mouth shut and your nose out of where it shouldn't belong and don't mess with me...or my uncle. Got it?"

"Uncle?" Josh gasped. "Lake's your uncle?" Nelson nodded. Now everything made sense—Thornton's partiality, Nelson's concern for the Thornton Valve, his interest in LakeCorps. "I guess you've pretty much got everyone in your pocket around here," he said, barely able to speak.

"You are quick-witted, aren't you?" Nelson said with a smile. "Wonderful! Don't worry. Everything will be fine. I guarantee it. Just don't cross me again like you did with that Dantell thing."

"I won't," Josh said, scowling at Nelson, "unless of course you give me good reason to. The best way to prevent my involvement in your affairs, Dr. Nelson, is to steer clear of me. You never know when I might get an urge to behave ethically." Nelson's eyes' widened for a moment, and Josh thought he could read fear in Nelson's handsome face. "You're not afraid of me, are you, Dr. Nelson?"

"Afraid? You keep your nose out this, Walker, or you'll find out what fear is." Nelson spluttered a few more threats, then turned without another word and left.

When he was certain Nelson was gone, Josh went back on

the roof for a while. The fans were just as loud as before, but somehow they didn't bother him as much. He sat staring at the lights of the city for some time, pondering the blue glow of the LakeCorps Building. It seemed much larger and less attractive than it had half an hour ago. His stomach rumbled, and with some regret and a little anger he realized that Nelson had failed to buy him another dinner.

The best thing to do for the moment, he thought, was to take Nelson's advice. Be cool, be quiet—just like Willowby, the nurses and most of the staff. Those who bucked the system got hurt by it, like Ravis. With luck, Josh would be done with his training in a year, and he'd have a ticket to go wherever he liked and do as he pleased. And if he encountered outright incompetence...well, he'd cross that bridge if and when he came to it.

Despite his decision, or perhaps because of it, Josh had trouble falling asleep that night. He kept seeing Dantell's face and hearing his frightened whispers: "I'm so afraid. I'm so afraid."

6

JOSH WOKE UP the next morning feeling refreshed: He'd only had one night call. He shave and showered, then headed to post op where a blocked bile duct was waiting for him. As he was talking to the ward clerk at the nurse's station on the fifth floor, Dr. Ravis walked up to him and drew him aside.

"Dr. Walker," he said, "I want to talk to you about a paper. I managed to get a six-month extension on my tenure decision, but I've got to finish a paper on amputations this year as part of my tenure package. Will you help me collect the data? It will look great on your record."

Josh hesitated, but Ravis kept hammering at him and finally persuaded him to accept. Another time sink. As if he had time to go to the bathroom, let alone gather data for someone else's paper. Still, he knew he wouldn't be politic to refuse the assistant chief of surgery. "How do I go about gathering the information you need? Do you have a disk?"

"What?" laughed Ravis. "This is St. Cahill's, Dr. Walker. We do things the traditional way, and let me tell you, it's a bitch. You have to go down to the record room in the basement, thumb through all the surgical records for the last five years, then pick out the records that fit the bill."

"That doesn't sound too hard," Josh said. "Just give me a list of patients and I'll assemble the charts tonight."

Ravis frowned and shook his head. "Damn it, you don't understand," he growled. "This requires time. You have to go through every record and cull the vascular procedures by hand. No other way to do it. My guess is that it will take you about...oh, two hours per file. Got the idea?"

"Two hours per file? For five years worth of files?" Josh glared at Ravis, dumbfounded. What did Ravis think he was, slave labor? He considered refusing, then saw the determined look in Ravis's face: His eyes looked cold enough to snuff our a lighted match.

Ravis turned to leave. "Meet me in my office after your rounds so we can discuss the details," he said over his shoulder. As far as the Swede was concerned, everything had been settled; Josh realized that he had no option but to give up what little free time he had and devote it to salvaging Ravis's career.

As he entered a holding room, he heard Nelson quizzing Willowby and the med students. "Mr. Simon will require a Whipple procedure for his blocked bile duct," Nelson informed his crew. "And just what is a Whipple procedure, Dr. Willowby?"

The intern coughed, clearly at a lack of words. "Well, sir, it was named for Dr. Whipple," he said at last.

"Brilliant, doctor," Nelson replied with a smirk. "Got any more information?"

"Allow me, please, Dr. Willowby," Josh spoke up, angry with Nelson for badgering the flustered intern, especially right in front of the patient, a small, older man who looked at the quarreling doctors with fear in his eyes. "The Whipple procedure is a surgical excision of the head of the pancreas and the distal common bile duct, along with a portion of the duodenum, presumably for a tumor blockage of the bile duct. The procedure was named for Dr. Whipple, a professor in New York City, who was the first surgeon to advocate this procedure for handling that type of problem."

"Very good, Dr. Walker," Nelson purred, smiling. Josh could tell the man was upset because of the hard way he glared at Josh, then at Willowby. "But next time let's have the interns and students participate in the recitations. It's good for their education, don't you think?"

"They can all read about the Whipple procedure tonight, doctor," Josh said. "For now, let's concentrate on Mr. Simon here. We want to give him our best."

Nelson flinched, and again he smiled his wide, defensive smile. Josh knew he was thinking about the Dantell debacle.

"Now, now, Dr. Walker, you know the outcome is always quite good. Look at Mr. Simon here. You have all the confidence in the world in us, don't you, sir?" Nelson patted the patient on the back, and Mr.

Simon smiled back wanly. "I guess so," he said.

Josh wasn't convinced. The more Nelson effused over a case, the more difficult it usually was. And Nelson's wild behavior during Dantell's operation was still fresh in his mind. Josh said nothing but hurriedly scanned Simon's chart. The chest X-ray and cardiogram were good; the lab work was okay, except for an elevated bilirubin and liver enzymes. Simon, a nonsmoker, appeared in good health otherwise, and Josh began to hope that this case might do reasonably well after all.

"I personally promise we'll take care of you," Josh said, patting Mr. Simon on the shoulder. The man smiled back.

Josh, satisfied that everything was in order, instructed the nurse to wheel Mr. Simon into surgery, then met Nelson in the O.R. to begin the Whipple procedure. Josh was relieved that Dr. Ravis would be there to guide them through surgery that might take from four to six hours in inexperienced hands.

Josh painted Simon's belly with iodine to kill the resident bacteria, then began draping the surgical field. When he was almost done, the circulating nurse came up to him and Nelson and announced, "Dr. Ravis can't come today. He has an important meeting with Dr. Thornton that can't wait."

"Oh, great," Josh sighed.

Josh looked up at the chief resident as doubt washed over him like a wave. Given Nelson's shaky track record, he might not be able to handle this tricky procedure without a very experienced surgeon to back him up. And if Nelson did fail, who did that leave to carry on and perhaps take the blame for a disaster?

"Hey, no problem," Nelson said cheerfully, as if he believed himself. When the suction was installed and the instrument trays brought up to the table, Nelson made his incision. A gush of bright red blood spurted from the wound. Josh suctioned away the blood as Nelson opened the abdominal cavity.

Just as Nelson set down his scalpel to begin the procedure, Dr. Se Su Wang, the anesthesia resident, peered over the ether screen and scowled. Josh knew little about Wang except that the man had a deep-seated hatred of the surgical department. Given some of the problems Josh had seen for himself in a few short months, he could almost understand Wang's fury.

"Dr. Nelson, I don't think a resident from this program is capable of doing this procedure by himself," Wang said. "You should be supervised by an experienced department member."

"Go pound salt," snapped Nelson. "Mind your own business and pass the gas. And try to stay awake this time, okay?"

Wang frowned over his mask. "I'll turn off the gas if someone doesn't come to supervise this...this butchery."

Josh felt his face grow hot. He scanned the room, wondering if the rest of the staff felt as embarrassed as he did. The nurses and other staff stood poised, as if ready to flee any moment. Or perhaps they were frozen in fear and confusion.

Nelson and Wang radiated anger. Josh could feel the heat of their hatred dispersing through the room like a mist. "Gentlemen, please," Josh said, in as soothing a voice as he could command. "There's a patient here who needs care. You can settle your differences another time."

"Fuck it, Walker!" grumbled Nelson. "Always such a wuss! This Chink's got it coming."

"Faggot," muttered Wang.

Before Josh could intervene, Nelson lunged over the ether screen, grabbed Wang by the head and fought him to the floor as the nurse anesthetist—a woman of great presence of mind, Josh thought—ventilated the patient.

Josh didn't break scrub, though he was tempted to grab Wang and Nelson by the collar and dash their brainless heads together. "What should we do, Willowby?" he asked the intern as the two doctors pounded each other against the floor.

"I dunno," Willowby replied. "This sort of situation wasn't covered in any of the surgical manuals I ever read."

"Well, somebody has to do something." While one nurse

tried to break up the brawling doctors and another ran for help, Josh began the Kocher maneuver, mobilizing the duodenum and the head of the pancreas. The later appeared to have a small tumor that was fairly well circumscribed and amenable to the procedure. Josh divided the duodenum and, with little difficulty, began the Whipple procedure. After what seemed like a very long time, Dr. Trench, the chief of anesthesia, entered and pulled apart the panting, cursing doctors. "You idiots!" raged the chief. "You and your squabbles! Your patient is on the table, doctors. Attend to him!"

Chastened, Nelson rescrubbed and appeared for the last part of the operation, although by then Josh had the situation well in hand. Blood trickled over Nelson's left eye and his face twitched with anger and humiliation.

"Glad to have you aboard, Dr. Nelson," Josh chuckled. "I don't think I could have carried on alone."

"Screw you," Nelson said under his breath.

After Nelson and Josh finished the procedure, Nelson got a call from Thornton: The young resident was to appear in the chief's office in five minutes. Josh was relieved; at least *he* wasn't going to be embroiled in inter-departmental politics.

"Shit! He'll eat me alive!" wailed Nelson. "And it's not my fault. It's all because of that stupid slant. Did you hear what he called me?"

"Get a grip, Nelson," Josh said. Nelson's egotism had always bothered Josh; now, combined with racism, the man's arrogance was more than Josh could bear. "Fortunately, you can tell Thornton that the operation was a success, and that's what's most important."

"Go to hell," Nelson said as he walked toward the door. "And don't you ever try to upstage me again."

That night, Josh felt edgy after he finished his rounds. Instead of eating dinner at the cafeteria, he went to a park nearby and bought two hot dogs, lemonade and a giant pretzel from a street vendor. As he sat on a bench, eating his food and trying to relax, he watched a boy of about ten race his dirt bike back and forth across the grass, oblivious of the signs all over which read NO BICYCLES in huge red letters. What was it about that kid, thought Josh, that reminded him of someone?

The helmet, the wheels, the disregard for authority—of course! It was Walt, a younger, more exuberant Walt, a future motorcycle maniac. At the thought of his friend, Josh felt moved to talk to him. If anyone would help him cope with all the craziness going on at St. Cahill's, it would be Walt. Maybe Josh needed the wind in his face as much as Walt did.

Josh returned to his room and searched through his clothes, looking for Walt's phone number. The former steelman had found himself a temporary job loading trucks and had rented a tiny apartment in Oakland. The number was on a scrap of paper in one of Josh's two pairs of jeans.

Josh was going to call when he was called away to emergency: a young white male with a gunshot wound in the thigh. An accident, he said. It was past midnight when Josh made it back to his room. Was it too late to call? Naw, Walt never went to sleep before the wee hours. Hurriedly he dialed his friend. "Walt, it's Josh. You still have your Harley, don't you?"

"Why, sure! You didn't think I'd sell my hog, did you?"

Josh laughed. Walt seemed to be in a good mood; maybe he had managed to control his blue moods. "Let's get together. Tonight."

A nervous chuckle rippled through the receiver. "Tonight? Are you kidding? It's half past twelve, man."

"Didn't wake you, did I?"

"No, Johnny Carson and I were just having a few laughs together. Don't you have to get up awful early?"

"Yes, but I need to see you. No, I'm not crazy." Josh thought about telling Walt his whole story, then decided not to. Why burden a man who had plenty of problems of his own? "Listen, I've had some hard times recently, and I need a fast ride on a motorcycle to clear my head. You with me?"

Walt paused, but only for a moment. "Yeah, I know how

you feel. I need a good tear every now and then too, buddy. Okay. Meet me outside Oakland Gardens on Louise Street in half an hour. You can't miss it. Me and the Harley will be out front."

Walt was true to his word. When Josh arrived at the tumble-down apartment building, Walt was sitting on his huge black hog, a glittering blue metalflake helmet on his head, a plain white one in his hands. It was a chilly fall night, and Walt had worn his pride and joy, a black leather jacket with a snarling panther embroidered on the back.

"You look every inch a Hell's Angel," Josh said, locking his car and walking over to Walt.

Walt laughed and nodded. "Here, take this." He thrust the white helmet into Josh's hands. "Gotta protect our brains," he explained, "or we might both end up in that slaughterhouse you call a hospital."

He was joking, Josh knew, but somehow he couldn't work up a laugh. Some of the fiascoes he'd seen at St. Cahill's were too close to Walt's assessment for comfort. "Come on," he said as he strapped on the helmet. "Are we going to talk...or ride?"

"Awright!" cried Walt. "Mount up, pilgrim. We're gonna hit the trail! I love this cold weather. When you get up to eighty or so, it feels like your face is going to fall apart."

While Josh mulled over the dubious potential for pleasure in such a situation, Walt kicked the cycle into life. The moment Josh settled into the seat behind Walt, his friend pulled the hog away from the curb and roared off down the quiet little street. Josh saw lights flicker on in apartment windows as they gunned past. "Where are we going?" Josh shouted, clinging to Walt for dear life.

"Hell, man, you think I know?" Walt shot back. "I just let the Harley choose the way."

They sped through Oakland, then up Fifth Avenue, strangely quiet because of the late hour. In front of the police station on Washington Boulevard, Walt slowed down to somewhere reasonably near the speed limit, then roared back to sixty as they passed the imposing black bulk of the Highland Park Bridge.

"Going to the zoo?" yelled Josh.

"Yup!"

"It's closed!"

"That doesn't stop me!" Walt shouted back.

The road that led to the zoo was as crooked as a local politician, and Josh felt his stomach racing around the curves ahead of him as Walt tore up the hill to the old entrance to the zoo, an area now used for employee parking. Only two cars waited in the lot. Walt parked his bike by the side of the road and crossed the street to a sturdy gate in a big chain-link fence. A huge lock and chain held the gate securely closed. Josh breathed deeply; the air stank of animals, dung and moldy hay.

"Don't tell me you intend to climb over that thing," Josh said, afraid that Walt might get himself into trouble.

"Naw, don't want to scare the animals," Walt mumbled. He led Josh along the fence until Josh became aware of faint snuffling noises on the other side of the fence.

"What's back there?" he whispered.

Walt laughed softly and pulled a squashed loaf of white bread from his gaudy jacket. "Beasties," he murmured. "You afraid? I didn't think doctors were afraid of anything."

Josh stared into the blackness, forcing his eyes to focus. Eventually he became aware of several pairs of glinting eyes staring at him, and then he heard a sound like the whine of a dying motor. A horned head, then another and another, pressed against the fence, and a pair of long white lips tried to seize his coat through the holes made by the thick wire. "Goats!" Josh cried happily.

"Yeah, pygmy goats. No bigger than a springer spaniel. This is the Children's Zoo, and these guys are the stars. Hey, back!" A feisty buck charged the fence and made Walt drop a slice of Towntalk White. Josh grabbed some bread and began stuffing it through the fence into the mouths of the hungry goats.

"This can't be good for them," he said, but smiled as he snatched more bread from Walt's hands. "Look how they jostle each other! You'd think they hadn't eaten in a week."

"Look at this," Walt said, holding a piece of bread up against the fence at chest level. One goat scrambled up onto her hind legs and snagged the bread with her long gray tongue. Josh and Walt fed the goats until the loaf was gone and the goats were reduced to licking crumbs from Josh's fingers.

"Yuck, goat slime," Josh said, wiping his hand on a tissue. "They're pretty cute, though, I've got to admit." He smiled at Walt, who was trying to pat a rambunctious doe. "You know, Walt, you're great. I would've never thought of going to the zoo, especially in the wee hours of the night. I feel...I feel like a kid again."

"No wonder," Walt replied, "they're all over the place."

Josh laughed. He couldn't control himself, and the laughter continued to roll from his mouth. Tears swam in his eyes and his chest hurt from the force of his laughter.

"Shush, the guards'll hear you," Walt said, but he was laughing too. At last they managed to stagger to the cycle and climb aboard just as Josh heard the sound of voices. Walt drove off, and stopped in a fast-food place a mile or two away. Josh ordered coffee, but he had a hard time drinking it; his laughter had turned to sobs, which he could barely suppress.

"It's so difficult at St. Cahill's," he confessed at last.

"Yeah, I know they work you hard." Walt had ordered a strawberry milkshake, and was now busily consuming it slurp by slurp. "Say, there are real strawberries in here," he marveled.

"It's not the work so much," Josh continued. "It's the deaths. It's so awful when one of the patients die."

Walt nodded. "Death is hard," he said. "I remember when my mom died. I was just fifteen." He took a pull on his milkshake. "You're not a kid anymore, Josh. You've picked a tough job, and you've got to stick it out so you can do what you were meant to do."

"Which is?"

"Help people."

Josh shook his head. "But...but they won't let me. Not the way I want to help, anyway." He told Walt about Dantell, McDermot and some other patients who had died shortly after surgery.

"Were they very sick?" Walt asked.

"Yes, I suppose you would say so, especially McDermot. But the others might have been saved."

Walt waggled his head. "Do you think the more experienced surgeons did the best they could?"

Josh paused, thinking of Nelson. He sure as hell wasn't experienced, though. "Well, yes, but the point is...."

"And people die every day in a hospital, even if they *might* have lived, because every surgery has risks, right?"

"Well, technically, of course that's true, but...."

"So...what's the problem?" Walt sat back and smiled. "You're a kid compared to those old carvers. Sure, I bet you've got some great ideas, and someday you'll be able to use those ideas. But for now you've got to take your licks and finish your residency. Then you'll be able to call the shots."

Josh stared at Walt, who now wore a thin pink mustache all around his mouth. Even Walt, with his delicate sense of freedom and his motorcycle and his midnight visits to the zoo didn't understand. Like so many others, Walt saw doctors as gods. Period. They couldn't do any wrong. "It's just not that simple...." he tried again.

Walt leaned forward and tapped Josh on the chest. "Y'know, pal, I think I know your problem. You need a girlfriend. That's it, isn't it? Ever since you and Becky split up, you haven't been the same fellah."

"This isn't about my love life!" Josh snapped, then lowered his voice when he noticed another customer turn to look at him.

He didn't want to think about Becky, especially not now when he was confused enough as it was. They had lived together for two years and had even planned their wedding ...until the evening Becky came home and told me she was seeing someone else. It had been a disaster. He tried not to think about her or women at all after that. "It's about doing what's right, about evil winning when good men do nothing...."

"You're losing me, Josh," Walt said with a yawn. "My advice? Try a diversion. Find a girl. Christ! It's two o'clock!" Walt pulled himself to his feet, clearly finished with the discussion. "I have to be at work at seven. How about you?"

"Six-thirty," Josh sighed. No use in beating a dead goat. He flung a five-dollar bill on the table. "Guess we'd better head back. This one's on me."

"Okay, but I'll take the next.

As they rode back to Oakland on the cycle, Josh felt the wind dig in his face and had to agree with Walt: He did feel as if he were about to fall into a hundred pieces.

7

THE NEXT DAY went by calmly enough. During his rounds, Josh visited Mr. Simon and was pleased to find that the patient was recovering very well indeed. He was alert and comfortable, if just a tad pale: a far sight better than the frightened, frail man who had awaited bile duct surgery just a few days ago. Josh felt proud to have had a hand, literally, in helping Mr. Simon's return to health.

Josh was about to enter the cafeteria when Nurse Dempsey came hurrying up to him. Although he disliked her almost as much as Nelson, he had to admit that she did have a fantastic figure. "Dr. Thornton wants to see you in his office. Stat," she said.

"Damn it!" Josh muttered. "Did he say why?"

Dempsey shrugged. "Does Dr. God have to have a reason?" she said, then turned to get into line ahead of Josh.

Josh rushed out of the cafeteria and headed toward the elevators. Thornton had probably heard Nelson's version of the donnybrook in the O.R. and had been led to believe that Josh was the cause of it. Or maybe Radcliff had blown Josh's suggestion about digital testing all out of proportion and worked Thornton into a fury. Whatever it was, he knew it couldn't be good. Worse yet, he had the sinking feeling he would not be able to distance himself from hospital politics, even in the short time he was going to be at St. Cahill's.

When he reached Thornton's office, Eileen smiled at him and ushered him into the chief's inner sanctum. Thornton was seated at his desk, but he wasn't alone: Opposite him, in a deeply-cushioned white leather chair, sat a distinguished-looking businessman in his middle fifties, a thin brown mustache darkening his otherwise fair face. The visitor looked up at Josh and smiled, exposing perfectly straight white teeth. Without knowing why, Josh distrusted the man immediately. It was the teeth, he thought. They looked as sharp and dangerous as the teeth of a shark.

"Dr. Walker, thank you for coming by on such short notice," gushed Thornton, rising from his chair.

Josh resisted a sudden urge to bow. "No problem, sir. I hope I can be of service." What did the old man want to see him about? Josh thought. And what was the sharp-man doing there?

Thornton gave a little laugh that sounded like distant thunder. "Oh, but Dr. Walker, you have already been of great service to us. I've just finished telling Mr. Lake all about your extraordinary skill and coolheadedness in the O.R. the other day."

Mr. Lake! Josh blinked. So this was the great benefactor-uncle Nelson had mentioned, Philip Lake, the chairman of the board. Josh had imagined a much older man.

Thornton introduced the two and they shook hands. "I hear you took over for Dr. Nelson when he became indisposed," Lake said with a smile. "Talk about baptism under fire!"

Josh nodded, though his mind reeled with confusion. Just what had Thornton told Lake? "Well, I just did what had to be done, Mr. Lake. Surely any doctor would have acted the same under the circumstances." Not that many doctors would believe the circumstances, he added to himself.

"That's not what I heard," Lake said, glancing at Thornton. "Dr. Thornton told me you showed exceptional poise, according to the chief of anesthesia. But what happened to Dr. Nelson? Some sort of attack or something?"

Josh looked at Thornton, who was staring straight down into his desk blotter, as if it contained some very important information. "Well, sir, I guess you could call it that...." Josh began, but Thornton cut him off.

"We're looking into it," he said briskly. "Dr. Nelson has been putting in long hours lately, but you know how driven our people are. I just thought you'd like to meet the doctor who so exemplifies the capable, professional staff that St. Cahill's is so well known for, ready to act at a moment's notice, no matter what the challenge."

Josh nervously raked his hand through his hair, embarrassed at the way Thornton was pouring it on, but noticed that Lake looked thoughtful and alert, as if he were eating up Thornton's every word. "Yes," Lake said at last, "you are to be commended, Dr. Walker. That's what we like to see at this hospital, action befitting the tradition of the long silk line. None of this high-tech mania, this over-reliance on computer systems. Oh, computers are fine, as far as they go, but they'll never take the place of meticulous handwork and good craftsmanship, not in surgical research, anyway. Right? If they did, think of all the people who'd be out of a job at my manufacturing facilities."

Josh gulped and felt the urge to loosen his collar. He already had something of a reputation for supporting computerization at the hospital, so how could he speak out against it? Lake might already know Josh's sympathies. "Yes, sir, basically that's right. However, as computer technology improves, there's no way of telling just how helpful it might or might not be to doctors and researchers."

A shadow passed over Lake's face, but only for an instant. In a moment he was smiling his fierce smile again, and again he praised Josh's quick thinking. After a few niceties, Josh was dismissed. Had he passed this thinly veiled test, he wondered, or failed? Or had he fallen somewhere in between?

As he returned to work, he couldn't get Lake out of his mind. The man had an obvious stake in keeping St. Cahill's in the dark ages in terms of technology and efficiency, and that bothered Josh no end.

In the cafeteria that night, pretty Lois Dorsinger joined him for dinner, a pleasant diversion, chiefly because of Lois's witty observations of the incompetence of the staff in general and Dr. Nelson in particular. Still, even she couldn't make him forget Lake's steady, predatory gaze and gleaming teeth. He briefly thought of inviting her up to his room to continue their talk, then dismissed the idea. Thornton might misinterpret the gesture, and besides, he was too exhausted to hold up his end of a conversation.

He dragged himself to bed that night, bludgeoned by the realization that in the morning Dr. God was performing one of his famous portal caval shunts, and Josh was to assist him as junior resident.

At 4:30 the next morning, Josh awoke from a disturbing dream of heart operations on goats, feeling groggy and dizzy. After a quick shower, he was headed toward the O.R. by 5:00, bone-tired but determined to look alert. As Thornton's assistant, he had to "warm up" Thornton's Black Box, an innovative apparatus designed by Radcliff for measuring pressure in the portal vein. Though Josh had never seen it before, its reputation for unreliability was legendary, despite Thornton's insistence that the machine was perfectly dependable; it had just never been adequately primed.

As Josh entered the O.R., he stared at the shunt device in disbelief. It fairly bristled with wires and knobs and dials, and reminded Josh of the Rube Goldberg machines he had seen in old magazines. As Josh started the power to the apparatus and began to set the various switches, he thought about the new computer system he had read about, a system which transformed analog data to digital read-outs. Such a system would have greatly simplified his job and made it much more easy to monitor the pressure readings. He wanted to be able to explain this to the chief, but decided against it; no way would Thornton listen to him, not after Lake's pronouncement the day before.

When he was finished, Josh gobbled down a quick breakfast of cereal and eggs and two cups of coffee, performed his rounds and returned to the O.R., where he scrubbed up alongside Nelson and Thornton. The chief was in a good mood, singing in the scrub room. "Oh, what a beautiful morrr...nnning," he belted out. Josh winced, remembering his days as an intern, when singing or whistling before an operation was regarded as a bad omen. He immediately chided himself for having such a childish notion.

The patient, Walter Rosen, was laid out asleep on the operating table. "Guy's a real wino," said Nelson, inspecting Mr. Rosen. "Looong history of cirrhosis. Makes W.C. Fields look like a Sunday school teacher."

"Stop it, Nelson," Josh said. "We've all got our problems. Even you." Nelson shot him an angry glance but said nothing more. Josh looked carefully at the patient's face. Although he was only sixty, Rosen's face was craggy and covered with wrinkles, making him look like a much older man. Josh felt sorry for him; even asleep his face was twisted in pain.

Josh prepped and draped the man's abdomen, and watched the scrub nurse, Betty Fenwick, assemble the instrument tray and equipment on the operating field. Rumor had it that Betty was one of the most experienced, competent O.R. nurses at St. Cahill's, as well as the entire city. Josh had heard that, during a bypass surgery where the resident had become violently ill, Betty had assisted the surgeon. According to the grapevine, she had done a far better job than the resident ever could have. "Dr. Thornton, we're ready," she said.

Thornton nodded. "Thank you, my dear. We will proceed. Is the pressure transducer warmed up, Dr. Walker?"

"Yes, doctor, ready and waiting," Josh replied. He wasn't the least bit groggy now; the coffee and the excitement of the impending operation had seen to that.

"Glad to hear it," Thornton said. "Pressure recordings are an integral part of this procedure."

In Thornton's hands, the knife blazed an incision from collarbone to pubis. To insure adequate exposure, Thornton made an additional incision, perpendicular to the original one. The abdomen was wide open, the skin peeled back like the top of a can of sardines. Josh noted that many of the internal organs were hidden by a grossly enlarged liver, protruding into the field like a huge tanker in a tiny port. "Christ, it's immense," Josh muttered.

"Quiet, doctor," Thornton snapped. "We have to get to the heart of the pathology. Let's measure the pressure in the portal vein."

Using tubing connected to the voluminous equipment at the side of the operating table, Josh and Thornton inserted a needle into the vein. A circulating nurse examined the ten dials. "Each dial is giving a different reading, doctor," she announced, fumbling with the numerous knobs.

"Adjust one dial and the others will adjust accordingly," Thornton grumbled. The nurse continued to play with the dials to no avail.

Josh watched, barely able to control his anger. Finally he could hold back no longer. "Doctor Thornton, this machine needs an analogue to digital computer program to insure accurate reads," he blurted.

"Nonsense, boy!" Thornton barked. "The apparatus simply needs more time to warm up. As I've always said, computers are prone to error and not reliable for this sort of delicate application."

Josh shook his head and stared at the humming machine in amazement. He knew the damn thing would probably never work adequately. As Thornton continued to jiggle the needle in the vein, trying to obtain a reading, Josh looked up at the gauges, but the machine appeared to have several minds of its own. The readings were all over the place.

"Stop the bleeding!" Nurse Fenwick demanded. "The abdominal cavity is flooding!"

Josh looked down at the opened abdomen. The chief's vigorous application of the needle had caused a large laceration in the vein, and the elevated pressure had promoted very brisk bleeding.

"Shit!" he whispered.

"My God!" Thornton blurted. "Get the blood started! We've got a major hemorrhage!"

Josh sweated through half an hour, during which Thornton finally brought the bleeding under control. No matter what else anyone could say about the man, Josh thought, he was a master surgeon, and Josh trusted and admired his skill. Finally the anastomosis began in earnest. Thornton mobilized the portal vein and began to join it with another major vein, the inferior vena cava. Since Josh had seen this type of procedure performed only a few times before, he looked on with great interest. "Miss Fenwick, where in the hell are my color-coded silk sutures?" Thornton said, scanning the equipment table.

The nurse looked up in confusion. Josh could see by the fear in her eyes that she was completely taken aback. "I...I thought you'd said you wanted to try the nylon sutures for a change, doctor. You said the other surgeons all told you that the nylon is much superior to the silk, and I thought...."

"Damnation!" Thornton roared, loud enough to wake the cadavers in basement morgue. "I never said anything of the sort! My dear, this is the long silk line! I have to have my silk! Nothing else will do!"

Jesus Christ! Josh screamed to himself. Delaying the procedure because of a god-damned piece of thread! Now he knew he had seen it all.

The circulating nurse raced to the workroom, returning with several large packets of silk sutures. As the scrub nurse laid them on the operating table, Thornton continued the anastomosis. When the swollen lobe of the liver protruded into Thornton's field, he yanked at the retractor to enlarge the exposure.

As he did so, the liver tore open. Blood gushed into the field.

Not again! Josh shook his head. This wasn't surgery; this was a joke. What was the matter with Thornton, anyway? He was a brilliant surgeon; how could he do something so careless?

"Whoa!" cried Thornton, as if he were trying to stop a runaway horse. "Let's stop this hemorrhage!"

Five gruelling hours later, the surgery was finally completed. Thornton appeared quite satisfied with himself that he had brought the hemorrhage under control and removed the diseased portion of the liver, although he had done it the hard way. It was almost as if he had created the disaster so he could play the hero and conquer it.

"Go ahead and close, Josh," Thornton said, bestowing on him the place of honor.

"Great job, doctor," Josh said, regretting the words as soon as they'd left his mouth. After he had closed the incision, he escorted Mr. Rosen to ICU and sank into a chair by the sick man's bed, his legs suddenly rubbery. No wonder: The surgery had taken ten hours instead of the usual three.

Josh was drowsing beside Mr. Rosen's bed when the night nurse roused him. "Mr. Rosen's in a coma," she said. "His urine output had fallen, and his blood pressure is sagging."

Still exhausted by 10 hours of exhausting surgery, Josh jumped to his feet, stumbled, and fell back into the chair. "Call Dr. Nelson at once!" He sat stunned for a few moments, then forced himself to his feet and began to work on Rosen.

After a while Nelson swaggered into the recovery room and assessed the situation, taking his time and making small talk with the prettiest of the nurses in attendance while Josh seethed. "You know, I saw this great movie last Tuesday, about this detective who...."

"How in the hell can you talk about movies?" Josh interrupted. "This man is dying."

Nelson fixed his blue eyes on Josh and gave him a look that glittered with disdain. "Well, Dr. Walker, since you believe you have what it takes and I obviously don't, you take care of Mr. Rosen. And keep in mind that Thornton doesn't like to see his patients check out feet first."

Josh glared at Nelson as the chief resident turned on his heel and stalked away. It was just like Nelson to leave at a crucial time, with the patient *in extremis* and Josh half dead from fatigue.

Josh tried to stabilize Mr. Rosen, but less than an hour later, bright red blood began pouring from the nasogastric tube.

"Holy hell!" Josh muttered to himself. "His esophageal varices are starting to bleed." This would never had happened, he realized, if that damn pressure transducer had been giving accurate readings. As Josh inserted a Blakemore tube into the patient to relieve the bleeding, a pint of scarlet blood gushed from Rosen's nose and mouth. Rosen suddenly went into cardiac arrest. Josh, Nurse Fenwick and half a dozen other nurses and interns worked furiously to revive him, but an hour later they knew their efforts were useless: he was pronounced dead at 2:05 a.m.

"Where's the family?" Josh stared blankly at the man's gray face, expressionless in death. It was the face of a patient doomed from the start, all because of faulty equipment, an arrogant doctor and a tyrannical chairman of the board.

"In the chapel," Nurse Fenwick answered, laying her hand on his shoulder. "Try not to take it so hard, doctor," she said softly. "We all did our best under the circumstances."

"Yeah, I guess." Her words brought him no comfort. All he could think of was Nelson, abandoning yet another patient.

Josh made his way to the chapel and found the Rosens sitting in the back pew, holding hands—his wife, two grown children, and a man Josh guessed was Rosen's brother; the resemblance between them was remarkable. Both the son and his uncle wore the long beards and wide-brimmed black hats of Orthodox Jews. Mrs. Rosen, a tiny woman with huge green eyes, stared at Josh like a deer that had just glimpsed a hunter. "Doctor...?" she whispered.

"I'm very sorry," said Josh, lowering his head, "but the news is bad. Mr. Rosen passed away at 10:05. I wish I could say something that will comfort you, but I don't know what to tell you."

Mrs. Rosen nodded as tears began to build up in her eyes. "Don't vorry, doctor," she said in a heavy Yiddish accent as she took his hand between her own. "God vill see us through. I know you did your best, such a nice young man. I can tell."

"*Yit gaddal, yit gadash...*" the two men and Rosen's daughter began intoning, and Josh recognized the words from a friend's funeral: It was the Mourner's Kaddash, the traditional Hebrew chant for the dead. Mrs. Rosen began sobbing on the shoulder of Rosen's red-eyed son, only a few years younger than Josh.

Josh hugged Rosen's wife, brother, son and daughter and tried his best to console them, but he couldn't help but think that this man, regardless of his alcoholism and damaged liver, didn't have to die. He might have been saved had Thornton been able to regulate the guage pressure.

Despite their grief, the Rosens were wonderful. They went from department to department, thanking every staff member they met for the heroic efforts that everyone had made on behalf of their beloved husband, father, brother. After they left in tears, clinging to each other, Josh stayed behind for some time in the chapel, motionless in the semi-darkness.

He tried to remember his childhood, when he went to Sunday school at his parents' church, but he was certain he had not learned very much there, other than how to start a ruckus that would thoroughly fluster the poor woman who taught his class. He had never considered himself a religious person...until this patient's death. Mr. Rosen's family clearly had some support system that went well beyond computers and transducers and anesthesia delivery devices. And their faith made him question the strength of his own.

"I just want to help," he said aloud, hardly aware he was speaking. "I don't give a damn about computers, except I know they could have helped Mr. Rosen."

From the corner of his eye he noticed a passing nurse stop and look up at him. For an instant their eyes met, and Josh realized she had heard him. He knew he had just committed the worst sin in the medical profession: admitting that doctors were not gods but mere mortals, just as fallible as the next guy.

Josh bowed his head into his hands and, for the first time in many years, began to pray.

THE RECORD ROOM was a huge, vault-like chamber in the basement of the hospital, stuffed with filing cabinets full of patients charts and records over the last fifty years at least. Josh sat at a small table, a dozen folders stacked up beside him, his head on his arms, exhausted but unable to give himself over to sleep. He had already been studying for five hours, but he just had too much work still ahead of him to engage in the luxury of sleep.

So much history crammed up in these cabinets, Josh thought, staring from one identical green file to the next. It was as if time had stopped inside the record room, and began again only once he was outside it. If only the hospital computerized its records! St. Cahill's was probably the last major institution in the city, maybe even the state, to keep nothing but written records. That was the influence of the old silk line, he told himself grimly.

Josh discovered that over the past five years there had been more than 300 vascular cases, most of which had led to amputations. Dr. Ravis had performed a fair share of the cases, but other surgeons had done a sizable number with similar results. It didn't seem fair to Josh that, after all that effort in the O.R., the best the patient could expect was an amputated limb.

No wonder the hospital wasn't in a hurry to make these records easily accessible.

One X-ray in particular had him stumped. It supposedly showed a compound fracture of the lower tibia with extensive vascular damage which had resulted in a foot amputation, but the X-ray itself was badly faded and stained. He wondered if John Johannsen, the chief of radiology, might either have another copy or be able to decipher the original.

Josh found a phone tucked away in an obscure alcove of the basement, called Johannsen's secretary and made an appointment for a short time later. When he was finished, he hurried to the chief radiologist's office, 10 minutes late, X-ray in hand. Strange noises, like the sounds of glass striking hard surfaces, came from behind the closed door. "What's with Dr. Johannsen?" he asked the doctor's secretary. "Is he pitching for the Pirates next season?"

"He's had some bad news," she replied. "But go on ahead. He's expecting you."

"Got a fielder's mitt I can use to catch some of those fastballs?" joked Josh, but the secretary didn't even look in his direction.

Josh knocked, softly as first, then louder, and at last a harried voice cried out, "Shit! Come in!"

Josh entered and found Dr. Johannsen sitting at his desk amid a disaster area. Crumpled paper and trash littered the floor, and shards of glass—once ashtrays and coffee mugs, Josh thought—lay in heaps against the far wall. "Are you all right, doctor? What's the matter?"

Johannsen snorted, picked up a miniature flower vase, hefted it in one hand, then set it back on his desk. He was a big, red-haired man with a red beard, and Josh would not have been startled to see him with a sword and Viking helmet, at the prow of a longship. "What's the matter?" the doctor said, in a surprisingly quiet voice. "Here, sit down. Let's have a chat. I'm so glad you came to see me, especially now."

Josh looked at him, unsure how to answer. He brushed the ripped up remains of a newspaper off a chair and sat down, carefully avoiding an overturned picture frame which lay at his feet. He was about to say something about rotten janitorial service when Johannsen spoke up. "They're trying to get rid of me, Dr. Walker," he said. "Asking for my resignation." Without a change in his calm demeanor, he picked up the little vase and hurled it against the wall, where it shattered with a smash.

Josh looked at the pile of shards, then out the window where the first snowfall of the season was dashing itself upon the glass.

"Sir, if you'd like me to come back, I...."

Johannsen shook his head. "No, doctor, I need you. Did I mention that the administration is trying to get rid of me?"

Josh nodded. He had heard stories about Johannsen and the radiology department, strange reports of patients receiving over 10 times the recommended X-ray exposure, lost files, hostile technicians and funds for new equipment that never seemed to show up in the department. It had all struck Josh as business as usual at St. Cahill's, but evidently someone had disagreed.

"It's all the fault of that bastard Regis Baxter, head of pathology," sputtered Johannsen, turning a glass paperweight over and over in his hands. "He's jealous because of all the funding that Radiology has received over the years. Why, did you know that he accused me of...." He stopped himself, smiled at Josh and replaced the paperweight. "Well, I don't mean to ramble on, Dr. Walker."

"That's all right, doctor," Josh said. He had no love for Dr. Johannsen, and he certainly hoped he would not get embroiled in this interdepartmental squabbling. What did Johannsen want from him? And what good could he do anyway?

"Here, I have something to show you. My secret weapon in my war with the administration." Johannsen rose and led Josh to a light screen used to examine X-rays. He withdrew a few from manilla envelopes on a table and positioned them on the viewing screen. "Here's a beaut," he said.

Josh peered at the X-ray, which showed two needles and a hemostat inside a patient's body. "My God!" he gasped. "Who did the surgery?"

"Dr. Thornton. It seems he left a few things behind after a gallbladder operation," Johannsen said, fairly cackling. "And here's another. That's a scalpel and blade and one of Dr. God's shunts, all under the liver." He pulled up yet another X-ray. "This is a Belfour retractor, blades and all, left in the abdomen after one of Dr. Ravis's vascular procedures. Guaranteed to inspire confidence, eh?"

"I don't know what to say," Josh muttered. It was hard for him to imagine such gross incompetence, let alone see proof of it right before his very eyes.

Dr. Johannsen looked up from the X-rays and smiled. "You don't have to say anything, my young friend. All you have to do is deliver these to Dr. Thornton, with my compliments. Look, I'll enclose a little note and seal everything in an envelope. You don't even have to let on that you saw anything. Deal?"

"I presume you think this will get you off the hook with Baxter and Thornton," Josh said.

"I don't presume, I know." Suddenly Johannsen ripped a sheet of paper off a nearby pad and scribbled a message on it. He pulled a huge X-ray envelope from a drawer and stuffed the note and the incriminating evidence inside, then sealed it and handed it to Josh. "Have a nice day, doctor."

Josh hesitated a moment. He hated to get involved in the doctors' private wars, but he knew he didn't have much choice. If he refused, Johannsen either get another messenger or maybe even delay his plan. Only a coward would back away from this situation. "All right, doctor." Josh accepted the packet and tucked it under his arm. "I don't know what's in here, of course."

"Of course," Johannsen said with a grin. "A harmless transferral of hospital documents. You're just doing me a favor.

I'm not exactly in any mood to deliver these right now, as you might guess. Oh, and by the way, I have the originals."

As Josh left the doctor's office, he thought he heard Johannsen laugh.

Josh was in Thornton's office before he realized he hadn't asked Johannsen about the X-ray of the amputation. Under the circumstances, perhaps that was just as well. "Is the chief in?" he asked the secretary, Eileen.

"No, doctor." Eileen shook her head and smiled. "Can I help you?"

Josh laid the X-rays on her desk. "Please just give him these X-rays. They're from Dr. Johannsen in Radiology. He said they were important."

"I'll see that he gets them."

A moment later, Josh left the office, his hands shaking. How could interdepartmental politics matter more than job performance? But at St. Cahill's, once a doctor got tenure, only politics mattered.

As far as he knew, a meeting to discuss Johannsen's status never took place.

That night, Josh couldn't get to sleep, despite—or maybe because—he knew that there'd be hell to pay in the morning if he didn't get any rest. After tossing and turning for an hour, he turned on his color portable television set and tried to watch Letterman. He was so tired he didn't understand half the jokes.

Just after midnight, someone knocked at his door. When he opened it, Lois Dorsinger, the junior surgical resident from Three West, stood in the doorway, her eyes glistening with tears.

"Lois! What the matter?" Josh took her hand, led her inside and shut the door. "Are you okay?" He guided her to the only chair in the room and took a seat on his bed, still holding her hand. He had always felt a special affection for her since they'd first met—not lust or even true attraction, as he'd felt for Becky, but respect. It was hard on her being the only female resident. She was always being hit on by her fellow residents and demeaned by doctors on staff. "What happened?"

"I...I'll have to start looking for a new position," she stammered as one tear slid down her cheek. "The chief and I...we had an...an argument."

"An argument with Thornton? They say if he argues with you he really likes you." Josh offered her a Kleenex.

"That's the problem." Lois took a deep breath and wiped her face with the tissue. After a few moments, she looked like her old self, but her voice still trembled with either fear or anger; Josh couldn't tell which. "We were in his office, discussing a paper I wrote, when...when he touched my breast."

"Shit!" Josh muttered. "That son of a bitch!"

"Wait, it gets worse. He began stroking my knee and thigh. I told him to stop, but I really think he didn't hear me. At least, it seemed like he didn't." Lois clasped Josh's hand tightly and paused for a moment. "Then he tried to reach his hand under my skirt."

"Jesus, I'm sorry that happened. It must have been awful. Did you call for help?"

"No, I...I slapped him." Josh winced. "In the face. And then I walked out."

Josh didn't know what to say. Lois had done the right thing, of course, but that wouldn't stop Thornton from trying to exact some sort of twisted revenge on her. "I suppose you could call his wife," he offered lamely.

"I thought of that," she replied. By now her voice was steady and calm, as if by merely talking about the incident she had thrust it further away from her. "But some of the nurses said the same thing had happened to them, and those who called his wife got the axe. Immediately. At least the others stayed on and he left them alone."

"So you might be all right."

"Except I slapped him," she said. "None of the others did that."

Josh laughed despite himself. "Sorry, he deserved it. I'm sure it's not the first time that old lech has been busted in the chops. Did you hear him say anything as you were leaving?"

"Yes, but I don't want to repeat it. I'm skunked, aren't I?"

Josh was about to say he thought there was a good chance the whole debacle would be quietly ignored when a loud whoop rang out in the hall, followed by the thunder of running feet. A moment later, a chorus of wild male shouting erupted from a distant room.

"What the hell is that?" Lois cried, automatically raising a hand as if to deflect a blow.

Josh realized at once how much the incident with Thornton had unnerved her. "Don't worry. Probably just the interns passing around the latest copy of *Playboy*. They're all jerks. I'll go investigate, if you want, tell 'em to keep it down."

Lois nodded. "Would you please? And do you have anything to drink, you know, like a Coke or Pepsi?"

Josh brought her a can of iced tea from the little cooler he kept in his room, then walked out into the hall to reconnoiter.

Above the racket of the interns' shouting and hollering came a strange sound, like an irregular heartbeat but much louder. Josh spun around and looked into the stricken face of a big German shepherd, its eyes protruding in agony, its mouth dripping with foam. The dog's right foreleg was missing, hacked off at its elbow. A circle of bone from the amputated limb glowed white in the overhead lighting. Blood flowed from the wound onto the green tile floor.

"Ohmigod," breathed Josh.

Shouts and drumming footsteps announced the arrival of a gang of interns, rounding the corner behind the dog at a gallop. "There he is! Thanks, Dr. Walker!" cried the jubilant young men.

Before Josh could speak, the tormented animal leaped forward and pushed its way past him, smearing his pantsleg with bright red blood. The interns pounded down the hall after it.

"What the fuck are you doing?" Josh screamed as they passed, but not one paused to answer him. "What is this, Frankenstein's lab?" he cried after them as they disappeared down another hallway, but he knew he might as well have been talking to himself.

"What's going on?" Lois was standing behind him in the hallway. When she saw the blood on the floor and on Josh, she gasped and fell back against the wall. "Good God! What happened here? Are you hurt?"

Josh shook his head. The hellish, the gruesome, the inexplicable—it was all part of the norm at St. Cahill's and no longer seemed as nightmarish to him as it once had. "Just another disaster. The interns' idea of fun. Carving up a helpless mutt without anesthesia."

Lois stared at him in disbelief. "Those bastards! We've got to report them!"

"Yeah? To whom?" Josh said. "To Thornton? You know about his sensitive nature first hand, don't you?" Lois stared at the floor. "This...this atrocity would probably strike him as humorous. Hell, look what he's doing to his patients with those damn Porta-caval shunts. I'll mention it to the dean of the school, but I'll bet they won't even get a reprimand."

Lois helped Josh clean up the blood with an old towel, then soaked his pants in cold water as he got into his pajama bottoms.

When Lois returned to her own room, Josh went to bed but was too shaken to sleep. Images of the tortured dog mixed with his memories of Dantell's face and the fear in the man's eyes.

Eventually Josh had enough and went down to the basement to work on Dr. Ravis's project. At the very least, he knew, it would help him numb his brain.

9

WHEN JOSH COMPLETED his research, he met with Ravis one afternoon in the doctor's office and handed him a thin sheat of notes. "Here's the data you'll need for your article, Dr. Ravis," Josh said. "I'm sorry I don't have better results for you."

The Swede looked up at him unconcerned. "What sort of results did you get?"

"Well, your vascular surgeries had a 50% rate of amputation, compared to 10% among other doctors at St. Cahill's and 2% nationwide." Josh stared at Ravis for a moment, wondering if the doctor had considered destroying the files. After all, they would be damning evidence against his tenure package. But Ravis didn't seem concerned. He only smiled, thanked Josh and shook his hand. Josh left the office in confusion. Denying all wrongdoing was a way of life at St. Cahill. Had he underestimated the doctor? Did Ravis intend to own up to the truth of his incompetence? That would be too much to hope for, Josh thought grimly.

As Josh made his way to the ward to begin rounds, he thought about the surgery he had helped Ravis perform just a week ago; if it were anything like business as usual, then it proved the records didn't lie.

The patient was from the "Gold Coast," the suite reserved for corporate executives and other worthies, most of whom made regular contributions to the hospital. The man, Michael Garvich, was one of Philip Lake's vice presidents, and Ravis had been under pressure to perform well, if not brilliantly. But Garvich was a slight man, and Josh was concerned. "Dr. Ravis, this patient's vessels are too small to accommodate the graft. The blood flow will be affected, and maybe even severely constricted."

Ravis, for reasons of his own, wasn't receptive. "Are you

saying I don't know what I'm doing, Dr. Walker?" he'd replied. "I've done over 50 of these operations, and I guess I have a pretty good idea of the correlation between blood vessel size and blood flow."

Except that only 30% of your patients make it through without an amputation, Josh had wanted to say, but he had kept silent and let Ravis use the oversized graft. After the operation, Mr. Garvich seemed to recover, but quickly fell ill again: Josh found that there was little or no circulation in the man's feet. He had to be brought back to the O.R. and, when the operative site was reopened, Josh saw at once that the graft was filled with clot and not functioning. Over the next few days, both of Garvich's legs became ischemic, and both had to be amputated. It was a terrible blow to the businessman, but to look at Ravis, Josh would have thought it was the surgeon who had become a paraplegic. "This could affect my tenure," he had complained.

Josh couldn't understand how anyone could be so petty. As he went about his rounds that morning, he couldn't get Ravis's pride and incompetence out of his mind.

A week after Josh dropped off the files, he met Ravis in the cafeteria. The vascular surgeon was all smiles as they sat down together at a table with coffee and Danish in hand. "I really appreciate you doing all that research for me, Dr. Walker. In fact, I've put your name on the paper I've submitted to the *National Journal of Surgery*."

"Well...thanks, doctor," Josh stammered. Was Ravis out of his skull? An article based on Josh's information was bound to hurt his career. "I've always believed that it's best to disseminate the truth, no matter how painful it might be. I'd really like to see the article, if that's okay. Do you have a copy of the final draft?"

Ravis coughed, nearly dropping his cherry Danish. "Well, doctor, as it turns out, the journal could only publish the work if I got it to them right away. They had a sudden opening in their December issue. If I hadn't sent it yesterday, I'd have had a long wait to get it printed. As it was, I barely had time to get it proofread." Ravis cocked his head apologetically, like a small boy who'd just thrown a baseball through a window. "You're not upset about that, I hope?"

Josh felt his jaws slack open, then snapped them closed just in time. Ravis had a reputation for being a tricky devil, and Josh wondered just how far he could trust the surgeon. "You didn't change any of those figures, did you?" Josh asked. Ravis avoided his question, and Josh backed off. Ravis was slippery, but surely even he wouldn't falsify such important information.

Ravis smiled but continued to hold his head at an angle, as if afraid to look Josh squarely in the face. "This article will be a fine feather in both our caps, Dr. Walker. Trust me."

Josh wasn't convinced, but he knew better than to question Ravis's motives. Instead he made some noncommittal answer, gobbled down his breakfast and excused himself.

Later, after his rounds, Josh got an urgent phone call from Dr. Cantini. "Dr. Walker, rumor has it that you actually want to do some good around here for our patients, for a change."

"What are you talking about, Sam?" Cantini must have heard about Josh's suggestion about testing the Thornton Valve.

"The walls have ears. Just meet me in Dr. Frieden's office at noon. I think you'll be glad you did."

Although he had promised to have lunch with Lois, Josh couldn't pass up Cantini's mysterious offer. The resident and the chief of the neurological section had something important to discuss with him, that was clear. Maybe it involved Ravis's paper, he thought, but whatever it was, the proposition was intriguing.

He told Lois he had an important meeting and dragged himself to Hal Frieden's office at the stroke of twelve. Cantini was already there, sprawled in an armchair, leafing through some diagrams as Frieden kept up an animated discussion with himself.

The chief of neurosurgery was an older man but still quite

handsome, with thinning gray hair and dark blue eyes. He took one look at Josh and jumped to his feet. "Dr. Walker, so glad you could come!" he cried, pumping Josh's hand. He sat down and waved Josh toward a chair.

"Is this meeting confidential, or is this just a friendly chat?" Josh said, taking a seat. "Dr. Cantini's invitation made me think I was getting involved in a plot to storm the Bastille or something."

"Nothing quite so drastic," Cantini said with a smile, "but interesting, nevertheless. And much more humane." He handed Josh the small bundle of diagrams. "It's a new instrument for treating acute pain in oncology patients and others." Cantini turned toward Frieden. "Tell him about it, doctor."

Josh saw Frieden's eyes light up with excitement. "With Dr. Cantini's help, I have developed a neurotransmitter, a special needle which can be introduced into the spinal cord. The needle is attached to a transmitter, which emits radio waves. Other types of this device are available, but they'd had some nasty side effects. Mine has none." He flicked his hand, as if brushing aside any potential drawbacks. "The radio waves sever the targeted nerve bundles without injury to adjacent nerve fibers, and all this is accomplished under local anesthesia, without an incision."

"Cool, huh?" Cantini said.

Josh smiled. Not only was the device a promising and helpful medical tool, but here at last were some doctors who believed as he did, who actually wanted to ease the pain and suffering of patients without regard to self-aggrandizement. "I'm very impressed. Do you have a prototype? Have you done any testing?"

Frieden and Cantini exchanged glances and grinned. "Yes, of course. We're not all barbarians here, you know. We'd appreciate your input and support, Dr. Walker. Come with me. I'll show you something."

The two collaborators led Josh into a small lab where dozens of white rabbits were kept in spacious cages. The facility was neat and clean, and all the animals seemed alert and in good health, though some were noticeably lean and others had lost some fur. "Every one of these rabbits is in an advanced stage of cancer or is suffering some other severe pathology," Cantini said, gesturing toward a bank of cages.

Josh peered at several animals closely. They gazed back at him, wiggled their pink noses in curiosity, then hopped to the far side of the cage. Up close, he noticed that some of them sported ugly tumors. "Remarkable!" Josh exclaimed. "Most of them behave perfectly normal."

Frieden nodded. "That's because they are absolutely free of pain, thanks to our procedure. Some of them are thin because they have no appetite, and others probably won't make it through the next few days, but at least they're not curled up in balls, thrashing and squealing in torment."

"Very impressive," Josh said. "I'd like to see what this device could do for terminal patients with acute pain. We have three patients with pancost tumors—you know, tumors of the lung that have extended into the axilla and are impinging on the regional nerves. They're in agony half the time. Your procedure would certainly be a blessing to them."

"That's why we asked you up here," Cantini said. "I've been running into brick walls trying to get some real cooperation between the surgical and neurological departments in this damn hospital, but with no luck." Cantini ran his hand through his thick, dark hair and sighed. "Everywhere I go I run into red tape and delays, and each department accuses the other of incompetence and graft. Each one has some valid points, but with Thornton dead set against cooperation and collaboration, there's a lot happening that's not in the best interests of the patients."

"That mule-headed Thornton!" Frieden snorted. "Sometimes I think he encourages dissention. Anyway, Sam and I thought you could help us break through the ridiculous rules and regulations so we can get back to the business of medicine around here."

"You came to the right man," Josh said, nodding. "I'll do what I can."

After the meeting, Josh tried to speak with Thornton, but the chief was out of town for several days. He did corner Ravis and Trench in Ravis's office, but both were pessimistic, to say the least. "I don't want the neuro boys invading the ward with some new gadget that probably doesn't work anyway," said Ravis pointblank.

Trench, the head of anesthesia, was less brutally frank but just as negative. "It would set a very bad precedent, Dr. Walker," he said softly. "You can't rush these things, you know. I'd have to talk with Dr. Frieden and examine his device in operation for a month or two before I could even begin to make a decision."

Josh sighed. His patients didn't have time for a lengthy delay; they were in pain *now*. Josh gave up on Ravis and Trench and approached several other surgeons, all with the same results. They were incredibly territorial, like wild horses circling around their foals to protect them from wolves.

That evening Josh realized he would soon be reduced to talking with Nelson, but he couldn't track down the slippery chief resident. He checked the cafeteria, the surgeons' lounge, even the nurses' lounge without luck. As was usual when anyone needed him, Nelson had managed to slide off the face of the earth. Even Nurse Dempsy hadn't seen him recently. Josh found her in the lounge, lighting a cigarette. "If you see him, tell him he owes me one. You know what I mean, doctor." She laughed and Josh turned away, disgusted, still in pursuit of Nelson.

Dragging himself up to his room late that night, he heard a soft sigh coming from behind his door.

What the hell? Had the interns stashed some other poor, dismembered animal in his room? Josh unlocked the door and turned on the light.

In his bed—in *his* bed—lay Sperling Nelson and Lois Dorsinger, side by side. Lois had pulled the sheet up to her neck;

Nelson lay sprawled on top of the sheet, a copy of *The New England Journal of Medicine* covering his lap. "What...what...what...?" Josh croaked. He felt his face grow hot and his throat swell in fury, making speech almost impossible. "What in hell? What are you doing here?" he squawked at last.

Lois closed her eyes, as if she were wishing she were someplace else, but Nelson laughed and waved. "Sorry, pal, I didn't realize you'd be back yet. See, Willowby is, uh...entertaining someone at my place, so I thought you wouldn't mind if we appropriated your room for a while."

"How...how...how...did you...?" Josh sputtered, mad at himself for showing his rage so plainly. It was bad enough that he had no say in the department of surgery, but it was completely demoralizing to think he had no scrap of private space he could retreat to and lick his wounds. "How did you get in?"

Nelson picked a heavy clump of keys off the nightstand. "You wouldn't believe how long it took me collect all these copies," he said, admiring his clandestine keyring. "I've got a key to practically every room."

Josh tucked his chin down on his chest so he wouldn't have to look at Lois. "That's really cheap," he muttered. "I can't believe it. Lois, do you know about this jerk? You do know he's screwing everything in skirts around here?" And maybe some in pants, Josh thought, remembering Se Su Wang's remark that had started the fight in the O.R. during Mr. Simon's surgery.

Suddenly Lois burst out crying. From the corner of his eye Josh saw her grab his own robe from the floor, jump out of bed and race into the bathroom. Josh got to the door just as she closed it. "I'm sorry, Lois!" he cried, knocking on the door. "Come on out. Please!"

On the other side of the door there was no sound but Lois's hushed sobbing. "I didn't think I'd make her cry," Josh said to no one in particular.

"It wasn't you," Nelson said, replacing the keys on the nightstand. "It was Thornton."

"What?" Josh turned and faced Nelson, who still lay naked on the covers. "Thornton? What did he do to her?"

Nelson shook his head. "Fired her."

Josh couldn't believe what he'd heard. "Fired her? But she's one of the most talented residents at St. Cahill's." He remembered what Lois had told him about Thornton's attack on her; maybe the old bastard had been afraid she would blow the whistle on him. Now it would be next to impossible for her to get another position anywhere else in the area, maybe the country.

"True, she's good. Too good for St. Cahill's. Actually, she tried to resign. That's when Thornton lowered the boom." Nelson fished a cigarette from his shirt on the floor and lit it with his lighter. "She was telling me about the whole incident, you know, crying about it, and we were holding each other and, well, we got carried away. You know how it is."

"Yes," Josh said. "I know. You took advantage of her. She was miserable and her guard was way down, so you stepped in and seduced her while her mind was too messed up to know what was happening."

Nelson took a big drag on his Marlboro. "Aw, fuck you! She's a big girl. She knew what was happening. Hey, look! I cheered her up. She was fine until you walked in."

"Yes, into MY ROOM!" growled Josh. Just then the bathroom door opened and Lois stepped out, fully dressed. Her eyes were bright red and lines of tears ran down her face, but she was no longer crying.

"I'm sorry, Josh. You're right about Nelson. He's a prick, but I make my own stupid mistakes, and I sure made one with him. I guess he told you about Thornton. I'm finished around here."

"What will you do?" Josh asked.

"I don't know, but I'm not giving up. I'm going into a new residency program somewhere if it kills me, and I'm not going to let that lecherous pig destroy me." She turned to look at Nelson.

"And I don't mean you, though the description certainly fits. Get your clothes on so Josh can have his room back."

Nelson flashed her a big smile and stayed right where he was.

"I don't remember hearing you complain," he drawled.

As Lois began walking to the door, Josh tried to take her by the arm but she pulled away from him. "Why don't you and I go for a walk?" he said. "You can tell me about Thornton, and I promise to listen." For the first time since his break-up with Becky, Josh began to feel attracted to a woman. Lois wasn't just intelligent and pretty; she was strong. He felt ashamed, knowing he didn't have one half her strength.

"Thanks, Josh, but I can't." She took his hand and squeezed it hard, and for a moment Josh felt incredibly sad. "I've got to get out of here." And then she was gone, leaving behind her pantyhose, which had a long run in one leg.

Josh stared at the door for some time, remembering Nelson only when the chief resident dropped ashes on himself. "Shit!" he snarled, slapping at his bare legs with his hands.

"Get dressed and get out of here, Nelson."

Nelson stood up and pulled on his boxers and pants. "No hard feelings, I hope, Dr. Walker. Say, how's Dr. Frieden's radio-controlled guillotine coming along?"

"What?" Josh spun around and watched Nelson slink into the rest of his clothes. He hated to admit it, but the resident was a good-looking guy, with delineated muscles and golden tanned skin. No wonder the women threw themselves at him. "How do you know about Frieden's new instrument?"

"Hey, c'mon, Walker. You're talking to *me*, remember?" Nelson smiled, his perfect white teeth glittering in the dim light of the bedside lamp. "I know everything around this hospital. It's my job. Now, I've heard Frieden wants you to help him get the surgery department to use his new, improved pain reliever, right?"

Josh nodded. In a way, he was glad Nelson knew as much as he did. Talking about the instrument helped him forget Lois.

"Absolutely. And before this...this debauchery happened tonight, I was trying to find you. You know those patients with the pancost tumors? I want to use Frieden's device on them. Will you support me?"

"I don't know, Walker. Those patients are going through holy hell and I'd like to help them, but shit! If that device doesn't work, our asses are on the line. The chief doesn't go for a lot of interdepartmental shit."

"I know, but I'm confident this will work," Josh said, striking the bed with the flat of his hand. "And what do those patients have to lose if it doesn't? Morphine isn't doing much for them. Christ, man! I'm surprised you can live with yourself, screwing your patients out of a chance for a last few painless weeks."

Nelson stabbed out his cigarette in Josh's empty water glass. "Okay, okay, Walker. But you'd better be damn sure of yourself. And if there's any problem whatsoever with the procedure, Frieden will have to stop."

Josh smiled in victory. Nelson ambled out the door as if he were leaving his own room, and Josh stripped the sheets from the bed. The whole room smelled of musk, and made him feel uneasy and alone. He'd open the window, he thought, despite the cold weather, and let the place air out.

10

Josh was taking a break during his rounds one morning when Dr. Cantini slapped down a copy of the latest issue of the *National Journal of Surgery* on the table in front of him. The magazine landed with such force that Josh's coffee cup rattled on its saucer. "What's the matter?" Josh asked.

Cantini picked up a corner of the journal and rifled the pages. "Seen this yet?"

"No, is Ravis's article in there?"

Cantini nodded. "I'm afraid so. I just want you to understand that I know you didn't have a hand in this travesty."

Josh grabbed the glossy magazine and flipped it open to the contents. "That bad, huh? Did he massage the percentages?"

"I'd say it's more like he took the percentages into a back alley and bashed them in the head with a baseball bat. But read it yourself. Alexander the Great never asked for a body count, you know. He rode out to the battlefield and personally inspected the slaughter."

What in God's name had Ravis been up to? Josh wildly searched through the journal. Dr. Ravis's article was in a prominent place near the front, complete with a photo of the good doctor in his surgical garb. As Josh read, he felt the blood drain from his face. His hands shook so badly he had to put the magazine down. "That slimy asshole!" he muttered. "He changed the 50% amputation rate that I calculated to 5%. And look! He says the mortality rate was 5% too, but I know it was 30%."

Cantini pointed to a paragraph near the photo. "I remember you told me you examined 60 cases. Ravis has pumped that up to 220. Makes him look like tough shit, all right."

"But it's dishonest!" Josh cried. "Blatantly, flagrantly dishonest."

"Well of course," Cantini went on, "what better way to kiss up to the tenure committee, especially after that catastrophe with Garvich? With figures this impressive, even the chief himself might get excited about it. This is St. Cahill's, doctor. Honesty is for other hospitals. Give us prestige any day."

"But my name is on that pack of lies!" Josh protested. "I should call the magazine and tell them the truth."

Cantini leaned over the table and stared into Josh's face. "You can if you want," he said, "but you'll walk in the morning. Think about your career, man. I have a debt of just over $200,000. I can't believe yours is much less."

"I think it's more," whispered Josh. He did some quick calculations in his mind and realized that, even with most of his pay going toward his loans, he still owed at least $300,000, and probably quite a bit more. It would be years before he could work off his loan...assuming he had steady employment. "I see your point."

"I hate to be the one to tell you this, and I know it's hard, but just let it lie," Cantini went on. "Concentrate on building the credibility of Frieden's neurotransmitter. Now that's a way to actually do some good around here, for a change." He stood up and leaned backward, as if to ease aching muscles. "Look at it this way: How can you help if you get kicked out on your can?"

Josh turned the journal face down; it seemed more harmless in that position, just another medical rag. The article still infuriated him, but Cantini's quiet logic had confused him too: Did it make sense to rail openly against the powers that be, or try to change things slowly, from the inside out? He didn't know what to do or how to think.

Cantini sat down and began eating his toast and fruit. "There goes the old charlatan now," he mumbled, nodding toward the front of the cafeteria. Josh glanced up and saw Ravis's back edging out the door.

In an instant he knew what he had to do. He grabbed the magazine and jumped to his feet, ignoring Cantini's soft yelp of surprise. He rushed to the doorway, darted through it and collared Ravis in the corridor. Waving the journal in front of Ravis's glaring eyes, Josh made a few false starts before finally finding his tongue. "Doctor Ravis, I am disappointed with this article," he panted. "Actually, I'm aghast. I'm enraged. Have you seen this? It's nothing but lies."

Ravis looked up and smiled nervously. He rubbed his hands together, then picked up the magazine and flipped to his report. "Well, I thought it was quite good," he murmured, smiling to another doctor hurrying past.

"But it's all wrong! The figures are wrong. They aren't the figures I gathered."

"We can't talk here," Ravis said, glancing around like a frightened deer. "Come to my office."

Josh followed Ravis in silence, fuming at the man's disregard for the truth. But who knew? Maybe Ravis had an explanation.

Once in the seclusion of Ravis's office, Josh threw himself into a chair and stared hard at the other doctor. "You do know that the figures here are pure bullshit, don't you?" He felt sweat run down his back and upper arms.

Ravis nodded, a peculiar sideways nod that Josh understood was common in Sweden. "Of course. I couldn't use your research. I would have lost all hope for tenure. I might have even lost my job. Look, it's publish or perish, Dr. Walker. Thornton as good as said that the first day you were here, remember? Trust me, no one will ever use this article for any practical procedure. It's basically just an image story, a recruiting article, a promotion piece."

Josh couldn't believe what he was hearing. "You mean it's all right to falsify data as long as it doesn't have a direct application in a specific procedure?" he asked. "Doctor, I saw you operate on Mr. Garvich, and believe me, it was *not* a pretty image."

Ravis shrugged. "Just a quirk of fate, that's all. And I certainly can't be blamed for what happened."

"You mean the amputation?" said Josh, mystified my Ravis's cryptic way of speaking.

Ravis looked at him with eyes not completely devoid of sympathy. "You haven't heard, have you? Garvich killed himself a day or so ago. A pistol to the temple. Seems he was quite the sportsman. Tragic! I told Thornton that the man should have had trauma counseling."

"What? Suicide?" The full scope of the situation was just beginning to strike Josh. He clenched the front edge of Ravis's desk and leaned toward the short, white-skinned man, resisting the urge to grab him by the necktie and force him to his feet. "Your patient committed suicide, and you don't feel responsible?"

"Please, stand back," Ravis said, frowning. Josh stood upright but continued to clutch the front of the desk. "Saddened, yes. Responsible, no. I'm a surgeon, not a headshrinker. I have absolutely no control over my patients' psyches. That's another discipline. I know it's hard being a doctor here, Walker. Someday, when you've been here as long as I have, you'll learn to put things in their proper perspective. It's every man for himself at St. Cahill's. It's the way things are and always will be here. And you'll see, this paper will go a long way to establishing a good, solid reputation for yourself."

"Good?" Josh exploded. "Solid? Are you joking? It's nothing but sheer fabrication, and my name is on it. People will think I engineered this fraud."

"No, because people won't know that the information is...um...exaggerated," Ravis said. He gave another brief smile that made Josh think of a cartoon weasel he had seen as a child. "The trouble with you, Walker, is that you take all this too seriously."

Josh didn't want to ruin Ravis, but the doctor's cavalier attitude made him furious. He felt his face "The trouble is, doctor, that I still have a shred of integrity left, though I'll grant you that it's getting smaller every day. People are losing limbs in most of your operations, and that sounds serious to me. What do you think would happen if the real documentation showed up in Thornton's hands?"

Ravis appeared unconcerned. He examined a letter on his desk, then looked knowingly at Josh. "I'll tell you what would happen. First of all, the article wouldn't be changed, challenged or altered. Second, you'd be out of this hospital so fast your head would be spinning for the next month. So don't get any clever ideas. All right? Have a nice day."

Ravis picked up his phone, and Josh knew their conversation was over. As he walked toward the elevator, Josh wondered why Ravis wanted tenure so badly, considering what it really stood for.

The rest of the day passed by in a blur. Josh conducted his rounds, helped out in emergency and wolfed down two quick meals in a few spare moments. Alone in the surgeon's lounge after emergency surgery on a homeless woman's slashed leg, he thought about what Ravis had said that morning.

The older surgeon really was holding all the cards. Even if he went to Thornton and the chief did believe him, Thornton would never risk the reputation of St. Cahill's by notifying the journal or trying to publish a retraction.

Josh poured himself a cup of coffee from a carafe beside the refrigerator. He dumped in four cubes of sugar and the remainder of a carton of half and half, then sat motionless, the steaming cup in one hand, the rolled up medical journal in the other. What could he do? The only honorable thing was to leave the hospital, but then, as Cantini had pointed out, what would he do about his loan? It would take months to find another position, assuming he could find one.

"Are you going to drink that, doctor, or just hold it?"

Josh started, nearly dumping his coffee on his lap. Next to him stood Lois Dorsinger, her face drawn and worn, her white coat rumbled and stained with yellow spots of iodine. Josh tried hard not to think about the last time he had seen her. "Tough day?"

"No shit," he said, trying to smile. "Here, read this." He showed her the article and she scanned through it.

"I can't believe this," she said, sitting down next to Josh on the green vinyl couch. She spread the journal out on her lap.

"I've observed Ravis in two surgeries, and both ended in amputations. In fact, one of those patients died. These statistics can't be right."

"They're not. I gathered the real data," Josh said. "Believe me, the real data is a lot different. It's a swindle, pure and simple." Josh turned toward Lois and laid his hand on her shoulder. He was no longer attracted to her, but in a strange way he still admired her. "I thought you were gone."

"I am," she said. She closed her eyes for a moment, and it looked as if she might fall asleep where she sat. "This is my last evening, then I'm out."

"And me?" he asked, still looking into her face. "Should I leave too? I can't take this...this bullshit anymore!" He gave the article a contemptuous swipe.

"Oh, no, Josh!" she said, grasping his hand tighter. "Don't leave. Who would pick up the pieces after Nelson? Seriously, it would be terrible for your career, and you have so much to offer. Once you're past this, you can go wherever you like and put all this slime behind you. Don't do it."

She sighed and rose from the couch. "Well, by rights I shouldn't even be here. I just saw you through the door and thought you needed cheering up. Didn't do a good job though, did I?"

Josh reluctantly let go of her hand. "You did a great job. I still don't know what to do, but you made me think some more about it. Whatever I choose to do, the answer's not going to be easy."

He watched her shuffle wearily out of the lounge, her head tipped forward and her back slumped. It was a hell of a place, he thought, to break a woman like that. It might even break him, too.

In the morning, Josh tried to forget about Ravis and the bogus article as he watched Dr. Frieden insert his needle into the necks of two patients with pancost tumors as Cantini stood by. Now this was exciting. This was what medicine was meant to be, thought Josh. After X-rays were taken to confirm the correct position, the mechanism was activated. Josh couldn't help but think of every Frankenstein movie he had ever seen: The procedure looked positively ghoulish. The patients, Mr. Apple and Mr. Schwartz, were in so much pain that tears streaked their cheeks, despite a heavy dose of opiates.

Josh examined Mr. Apple first. At first he felt no effect from the needle, but when Frieden increased the current, the patient began to relax and a look of contentment washed over his face. Josh reached out and took his hand. "Well, Mr. Apple, how is it working now?"

"Gee, doctor, I feel okay!" the man said, euphoric in his disbelief. "I barely feel any pain at all. It's like it's sitting behind me, waiting for me, but it's not touching me."

Mr. Schwartz had similar results: once the current was increased, his pain seemed to disappear. "God bless you, doctor," Schwartz said, gripping Josh's hand in a fierce handshake.

"Hey, Dr. Frieden and Dr. Cantini here deserve the credit," Josh said, nodding toward the doctors. "I just asked them to do it." He turned to face Frieden. "Wonderful job, doctors. It looks as if their pain problems may be solved for good. Sure beats having to take opiates every two to three hours, doesn't it, Mr. Schwartz?"

The elderly man nodded, clearly relieved. "They didn't work so good."

"Gentlemen, your pain won't return," Frieden said, looking from one patient to the other as he spoke. "Guaranteed."

Josh slapped Frieden on the back. "We have other patients who could benefit from this, you know."

"Bring them on," crowed Cantini.

Later that morning, Frieden performed the procedure on two more patients, who were just as relieved and happy as Apple and Schwartz. As the days passed, Dr. Frieden was proven correct; Josh let him perform the procedure on several other terminal patients, with similar levels of success. Josh was ecstatic. This was why he had studied surgery in the first place, for results like this.

So when Dr. Thornton returned the following week and summoned Josh to his office, Josh wasn't concerned. He figured the chief was going to commend him and Frieden for such excellent work, but when he saw Thornton's angry expression he realized the truth: Thornton cared less about medical care than departmental protocol.

"Dr. Walker, just what the hell is going on in the surgical ward?" barked the chief. His face was as red as his power tie and his hands were clenched in fists. "I leave for one week and what do I find? The neurosurgical department is...is *experimenting* on my patients. What are they doing, anyway? Black magic? Bunch of Druids!"

Josh resented Thornton's angry put-downs. "Sir, those patients...."

"God damn it!" Thornton spat. "You're more dense than I realized, Walker. I don't care if they're resurrecting the dead. This is the *surgery* department, and don't ever forget it. If this kind of disruption ever happens again, I'll personally kick your ass right out the door. Get me?"

Josh bristled. It didn't seem to matter at all to Thornton that his patients were being helped. "But sir, the patients got almost total pain relief, with...."

"Enough of this, Dr. Walker," Thornton said, recovering his professional demeanor. "We are not here to offer our patients as experimental animals for the neurological department. If Dr. Frieden wants to test his toys on his own patients, so be it, but not on mine and not in my department. Have I made myself perfectly clear?"

Josh nodded, but Thornton wasn't done speaking. He went on for several minutes, lambasting Frieden and the neurological department. After a while, his stern expression softened, he clasped his hands in front of him and began to talk in a fatherly tone. "It's not that I'm against progress, mind you," he said, looking into Josh's face. "I read that article Dr. Ravis wrote with your help, and I want you to know I was very impressed."

Josh hesitated, not sure whether or not he should mention that Ravis had cooked the statistics. "Sir, that article was... misleading and never should have been published," he began.

"Nonsense!" Thornton leaned back in his leather armchair, a look of satisfaction on his face. "I know what you're about to say. You're going to tell me that Ravis doctored the percentages, so to speak. You think I don't know that?"

"You know? I...I can't believe...." He sounded like an idiot, but Thornton had completely taken him by surprise. It had never occurred to him that a man of the chief's stature was in collusion with Ravis. "I never presume what anyone might or might not know, doctor," he said at last.

"A wise move," Thornton agreed. "The only reason I'm bringing this up is because I need an article on the Thornton Valve for the surgeon's conference coming up in April. I have Dr. Radcliff working on a paper already, but I'm sure he could use some help with the research and writing."

"The Thornton Valve?" The salvage rates were so bad on the cases involving the notorious valve—5% success or so, he guessed—that Josh knew Thornton must have intended to make up his own percentages. "Sir, the device just hasn't been used enough to warrant an article of any...."

"80 cases," Thornton interrupted. "Maybe 90. With an 80%, hell, a 90% success rate. That sounds good, doesn't it?" Josh shook his head. He was beginning to see that reality was whatever the chief wanted it to be. "Look, Dr. Walker, I know you're not a fool. You know and I know that the Thornton Valve isn't worth shit, but I've got several mill in grant monies coming in from the state resting on this damn valve, so I've got to do something. The editor of *Modern Surgery* owes me one."

"But to falsify case results so blatantly...it would do more harm than good if you were discovered," pleaded Josh, trying to persuade Thornton to drop the whole idea. "It could be conceived of as a criminal deception if the information of falsification fell into the wrong hands." Even as he spoke, Josh knew Thornton was aware of all he said.

"Don't worry about me, son," Thornton replied. "I've got my ass covered. Now in the morning you report to Dr. Radcliff and tell him I sent you."

Josh all but ran from Thornton's office, his face burning with fury and shame. He hated the idea of working on yet another fraudulent paper, but he had no choice? He didn't even have the gumption to refuse Ravis; how could he work up the courage to tell the chief to stick it in his ear?

He was so immersed in his rage and confusion that he almost didn't see the two men in a side corridor, but he clearly heard them, their words soft but urgent. What finally made him look and listen more carefully was the sound of a particular voice, a fine, polished voice he had heard just once: the voice of Philip Lake. For some reason he couldn't quite understand, Josh hung back and stopped, focusing in on the conversation.

"Damn it, Alan!" Lake said. "You've got to pay it back. Can you imagine the bad press? God, how could you have been so stupid!"

"But Phil," whined the other man, "these guys I owe, they're pretty tough. If I didn't pay them, I'd be fishbait by now."

Josh drew a deep breath. If he didn't know better, he'd have thought he had stumbled into some kind of espionage movie. Who was this Alan character, and why was Lake so concerned about his money problems?

"Who says you're not?" Lake growled. "Hell, I didn't even know you had a problem." Lake gave a nervous laugh. "Why don't you go to the sixth floor? Maybe the mental health department can help you out. Or maybe you should join Gamblers Anonymous. You need to do something."

"I don't need help. I need cash, and I need it now," Alan said, his face becoming moister and redder by the moment. "Come on, Phil, lend me the money," Alan insisted. "It's just small change to you."

"What? Are you crazy? Small change? You'd never be able...."

Suddenly Josh became aware that his shadow was protruding down the hallway. The men had to have noticed him. With as much speed as he could muster, he ran to an exit and plunged down the stairs, stopping three floors below. In the hallway, he paused to catch his breath as a nurse walked by, staring at him. "Exercising, doctor?" she asked.

"I guess so," he gasped.

"Some of us walk up and down the steps during lunchtime," said the woman. "Helps burn up the weight. At least, that's what *Cosmo* says."

"Um, that's right," Josh answered, trying to look interested. After a little more small talk, the nurse walked on and Josh slumped against the wall. What in hell had made him run away from Lake and the other man? He hadn't done anything wrong, and as far as he knew the chairman had been arguing about some relatively minor matter. No, he had every reason to be wary. There was something in the tone of Lake's voice, the soft, cruel edge of it, that had made Josh run. From what he wasn't sure, although the words *gambling*, *debts* and *fishbait* all in the same conversation didn't indicate anything good.

Josh took a deep breath, then another. What was he thinking? He had to put this incident out of his mind and get on with his life. The last thing he needed was more turmoil.

11

A WEEK DRAGGED by like a year. Cold, snowy weather had set in, and Josh realized that, for all his running from ward to ward and O.R. to O.R., he was gaining weight. When he mentioned this to Cantini one day, the young resident had an answer: "Racquetball. I'll teach you. It's easy. I reserved a court at the Racquet Club in Oakland tonight so I could work on my serve, but you and I can bat the ball around together instead. How does 7:30 sound?"

"But...but I don't have a racquet or any other equipment," Josh said, a little embarrassed. He'd never played any racquet sport before and had no idea what sort of gear might be needed. "Besides, I don't know if I can find someone to cover for me during the night. And I know my car will never make it through the snow."

Cantini winked at him. "They'll rent you everything you need," he said.

For the first time Josh noticed Cantini's warm brown eyes that shone with genuine good humor. They were good eyes for a caring doctor. Josh could feel himself relenting. It sounded like fun. "What does it cost?"

"Five bucks or so, more if you need goggles," Cantini said. "And I'll personally find you a replacement for tonight, pick you up in front of the hospital *and* drive you home. You just ran out of excuses, doctor."

Cantini was as good as his word. Not only did he teach Josh the rudiments of what turned out to be a very basic sport—hit the ball in such a way that your opponent can't return it—but, when the people who had reserved the court failed to show up, Cantini continued his lesson, teaching Josh to perform a lethal forehand slam. "I only wish I could use this on Thornton sometime," Josh laughed, envisioning Thornton's face on the wall as he returned Cantini's serve as hard as he could.

"And Ravis and Nelson and Radcliff," Cantini added. "What a bunch of incompetents!"

The lesson slowly transformed into a regular game, in which Cantini massacred Josh 21 to 5. Josh couldn't believe that he was winded and sweating like a galley slave, while his colleague looked as if he had barely worked up an appetite.

After they'd showered and dressed, Josh invited Cantini out for a beer at the lounge across the street. Over Iron City, Josh poured out his problems with Thornton and the bogus paper he wanted Josh to write.

"Why aren't I surprised?" said Cantini, gulping his beer. "That maniac! After the way he totally discounted Dr. Frieden's work, I'm surprised the entire neurology department just doesn't pack up and leave."

"I feel terrible about Frieden and the neurotransmitter," muttered Josh. "I wish I could do something."

"But you did." Cantini patted Josh's hand. It was one of the few friendly gestures anyone had made toward him since his arrival at St. Cahill's. "It's not your fault. You did all you could. And you'll be glad to know that Dr. Frieden hasn't given up, but is secretly negotiating to use the neurotransmitter at another hospital."

"My God!" Josh gasped. "I guess St. Cahill's deserves what it gets. Thornton's an idiot for letting a godsend like that slip through his hands. If I write something positive about that valve, Sam, I'll be implicated in a scandal. Wait till you see the brouhaha that will take place the minute anyone outside of this madhouse sees how truly worthless that device is."

Cantini stroked his chin, deep in thought. "I see your predicament. That frigging valve hasn't worked right yet. If anyone but Dr. God himself were trying to install it, he'd be out on his ass faster than you could spit."

"The problem is," Josh said, running his forefinger up and

down the handle of his beer stein, "that they haven't tested the thing, at least, not properly. Radcliff doesn't have a dog lab, and whatever tests or examinations he is running sure don't seem to hold much water. The leaflets are always sticking, and then he and Thornton blame the engineers. I think it's a design problem, pure and simple. The damn thing just doesn't work and never could."

Cantini leaned forward. "How would you like to prove it?"

"Prove it?" Josh echoed. "I'd love to! But how?"

"Ever hear of Elmo Elberkann?"

Josh grinned weakly. "Didn't he pitch for Atlanta?"

"Funny, Dr. Walker." Cantini pulled a pen from his breast pocket, slipped the coaster from under his glass and began to scrawl something on the soggy paper. "Dr. Elmo Elberkann, at Kingston Andrews University. The Khan, they call him for short, but he's really a nice guy, a puppy dog."

Josh took the coaster from Cantini and turned it round and round in his hands.

"The Khan, huh? Sounds dangerous. What does he do?"

"He's the city's foremost authority on flow theory, computer graphics and mathematical modeling of physiologic systems, that's all," Cantini said, slowly, as if trying to make each word sink into Josh's weary brain. "And he's one of Frieden's best buddies. If you want, I'll ask Frieden to write you a letter of introduction, you know...subtly explain all the shit that's going on here and how you're trying to expose it."

"I'm not trying to expose it," Josh objected. "I'm just trying to make sure that I'm not the one covered in shit when it does hit the fan."

"Apt analogy," Cantini said. "So what do you think? Is it a go? Should I tell Frieden? You don't have to take Elmo out on a date or anything...just talk to him.

"Great!" snorted Josh. "I can see it now. `Dr. Thornton, I want to talk to this guy to find out how to test your valve and prove it's a fake.' I don't think he'll go for it."

"Of course not, not if you actually tell him the truth." Cantini rolled his eyes. "Haven't you learned anything? You really are a babe in the woods. First of all, you don't have to tell Thornton anything. Make up some excuse if you find yourself spending a lot of time with Elmo. If Thornton presses you about your absences, tell him you're taking classes at Kingston Andrews to learn more about flow theory and enhance the credibility of his damn valve. Tell him you need to know more about flow theory in order to intelligently discuss the brilliant design of the device. You know, suck up to him. He'll be peeing his pants, he'll be so happy."

Josh realized right away that Cantini was right. Thornton was an egomaniac. If Josh could just approach him in the right way, with enough flattery, he could probably bamboozle the chief into almost anything. "Do you think this Khan guy will want to help me test the valve, even though I'll have to tell him it's all on the sly?"

Cantini shrugged. "Hell, don't ask me! Ask him. You wanted my advice, I gave it to you. If anyone in this city can help you find a way to test that fucking valve, it's The Khan. Whether he'll help you do it or not...well, that's another story."

"Hey, easy!" Josh laughed. He picked up his glass stein and gulped down the last of his Iron City. "Sure, I'll give it a try. Ask Frieden to go ahead and write that letter. What have I got to lose?"

"Other than, of course, your residency."

"Well, yes." Josh frowned, then shook his head. "At this stage, I'm not sure that would be such a great loss."

"Dr. Walker, have a seat," boomed Thornton. He was obviously in a good mood, and Josh intended to take advantage of it. "I got your message that you wanted to discuss...." He rummaged for a piece of paper on his desk, found it, studied it, and stared back at Josh. "A class?"

"Yes, doctor, a class on flow theory. I've called Kingston Andrews, and they do offer a course, taught by a Dr. Elberkann. Dr. Frieden wrote him a letter, recommending me. I thought I could audit the course. That way it would be free."

Thornton frowned as he flipped the note into his wastebasket. "A class on flow theory? I don't understand."

Josh took a deep breath. He felt a strange hollowness in the pit of his stomach. Maybe he had overestimated the size of the chief's ego. "Well, since I've begun working with Dr. Radcliff on this journal project, I've discovered that I'm lacking a lot of technical information that I need to know in order to thoroughly explain how the Thornton valve works. Dr. Radcliff just doesn't have the time to discuss the fine points with me. So when...."

A transformation came over Thornton. Josh watched as the chief's face lit up with sudden understanding and his eyes glowed with self-indulgence. No, Josh thought grimly, he had not been mistaken about his boss's pride. "Now I understand," Thornton said, in as jolly a voice as Josh had ever heard him use. "You want to walk the walk and talk the talk."

"Yes," Josh said gratefully.

"You want to be able to understand and explain any technical complexities that might arise in the examination of the valve, and perhaps in any questions that result from the article," Thornton continued. He sat back in his chair and folded his hands behind his head, the picture of relaxation.

"Exactly," Josh sighed, relieved that the old man was playing into his hands so easily. He sat back in his chair too.

"With such advanced theory at your disposal," Thornton went on, "you would no doubt discover ways to enhance the performance of the valve."

Suddenly the room felt very hot. Josh felt his hands become soft and damp. What was Thornton's angle? "I suppose so," he said carefully. He must be careful not to reveal his true purpose. "I guess what I learn could be used to develop a new, more efficient valve. But surely that's not material for this article."

Thornton shook his head and gave a very tight smile that made Josh feel incredibly uncomfortable. "You misunderstand me, Dr. Walker. Making the valve more efficient isn't necessary.

What is necessary is convincing the medical world that the valve actually works. If you take these classes, I'm sure you'll find out all sorts of wonderful things to say about the Thornton Valve, regardless of their present veracity."

"Huh?" Josh said, startled out of his comfortable position. The word slipped out of his mouth before he had a chance to gather his wits. "I'm sorry, I think I misunderstood you. Could you say that again?"

Thornton's smile vanished and his face began to tighten like a vise. "Oh come now, Walker! You understand just fine. Must I make myself plain? All right. Go ahead and audit this class, but use it as a fact-finding mission. If you should happen to find out any information that will make the valve appear in a better light, then you have my permission to...ah...massage the facts a little to give the valve the best credibility possible."

Josh inched forward until he was sitting on the very edge of his chair. He had thought he'd seen and heard every low trick possible at St. Cahill's, but evidently Cantini was right. He was a babe in the woods when it came to misrepresenting the truth. "Doctor Thornton, let me get this right," he said. "You want me to invent some capabilities and benefits of the Thornton Valve? Whether or not they have any basis in reality?"

Thornton nodded. "Sure. There's simply not enough hard evidence to prove you wrong, so you can pretty much say what you like. It will be years before anybody can perform the experiments necessary to refute you or substantiate you, and by then the valve will be redesigned."

"Doctor, I can't do that," Josh gasped, still reeling from what Thornton was asking of him. "Falsifying results is bad enough, and don't ask me to do that either. But fabricating results from sheer speculation....It's not only unethical, it's illegal *and* immoral."

Thornton shook his head, as if he were responding to a very dull child who hadn't caught on to a simple homework problem. "Dr. Walker, you can't expect to get up on a moralistic high horse and get anywhere at St. Cahill's. We need to get our job done here, and we get it done whatever way works best for us. I've got to justify the money that's gone into this valve, and damn it! That's what I'm going to do. Now are you with me?"

Josh teetered on the verge of an angry outburst, finally realizing that his rage wouldn't solve anything. In all likelihood, it would only make Thornton suspicious, and that was the last thing Josh wanted to do. He clenched his hands together and forced out an answer he didn't like to say. "I'll take it under consideration," he replied. "It might be that these classes won't pose any opportunities for...the "benefits" you have in mind. First I have to get the professor's permission to audit the class."

"Attaboy," Thornton said. "You do that. Of course, you'll be missing a lot of work. You'll have to arrange substitutes."

"I can do that," Josh answered. He was in a hurry to leave the office, and fortunately Thornton was in no hurry to keep him. Abruptly, for no reason Josh could see, Thornton broke off in the middle of a sentence and excused himself, saying he had to make a phone call. It was just as well as far as Josh was concerned; he didn't know how much more he could take.

A week later Josh found himself driving across town in a downpour of sleet and freezing rain to keep his evening appointment with Elmo Elberkann of Kingston Andrews University's engineering school. As he drove, Josh thought about how lucky he was to have found another resident to cover for him, so he would have time to go over his situation at length. He suspected that Frieden and Cantini had helped arrange a substitute.

Josh arrived on campus just as evening classes were letting out. The science hall was old and ornate, pale yellow brick with dark green woodwork and thistles carved in stone above the door.

Why thistles? It took Josh a moment to remember that Donald Andrews, the university's cofounder, was a Scot. There was something stately and comforting about the building, which reminded Josh of an aging professor from the Old

Country. Not exactly high-tech quarters for an engineering school, he mused, but then, he preferred the slightly shabby buildings to the hard steel and glass of St. Cahill's.

The hospital felt and looked more like a fortress, stark and boxy; no thistles there, no need for symbolism. It was a citadel against death, a stronghold offering protection, complete with surgical knights in armor, for the sick and dying. At least, that was what Thornton probably liked to believe.

He climbed a daunting flight of stone steps and went inside. The dark tiled halls of the science building rang with footsteps and loud discussion from scores of students walking home, unchaining bicycles and generally milling about outside classrooms. Josh marveled at the fact that these students were used to a schedule, a distinct starting time and quitting time. Classes lasted three hours; when the bell rang, that was it. There were dismissed. Not so at the hospital. You stayed and worked until the patients' needs were satisfied. It was a life and death situation, and under those circumstances time had no meaning.

Josh drew a sheet of paper from his pocket and followed the directions up a flight of stairs and down a narrow hall to an office door: 213. He paused with his hand upraised, frozen in the act of rapping on the door. *This can't be a good idea.* What would an engineering professor understand about hospital politics? He hadn't even seen Frieden's letter of recommendation, and he wondered what Frieden had told his friend, The Khan.

As he was standing still, contemplating turning back, the door opened and Josh found himself staring into a rugged, virile face lit up by bright blue eyes and a melancholy smile. A shoulder-length mane of gray hair framed his massive forehead and high cheekbones. "Dr. Walker?"

Well, he certainly didn't look like a merciless barbarian. Josh extended his hand. "Yes, and you must be Dr. Elberkann. Call me Josh, please."

"Everyone calls me El," the professor said, "That is, my friends do."

"Well, count me in that category." Already Josh liked the soft-spoken scholar. El invited Josh into his office and offered him coffee and Oreo cookies. "I haven't had dinner yet," El apologized, stripping a blue wrapper from a small package of cookies.

"I'll pass, but go right ahead." For several minutes they exchanged pleasantries, talking about life at the hospital versus life at the university, and Josh realized that Elberkann probably encountered just as much in the way of sleazy politics as any doctor did. "Academics are especially vicious," he remembered Cantini telling him once.

"El, I know you're busy, and I appreciate your taking the time to talk to me, so I'll try to be concise. The chief of surgery at St. Cahill's has developed a heart valve that, I believe, has serious flaws. The survival rate is very low."

"Hal mentioned `potential problems' in his letter," El said, nodding. "Do you think he meant this valve?"

Josh cleared his throat. He had to be careful what he said next; after all, he didn't want to appear as if he was badmouthing his own chief of surgery. "The trouble is that the valve has not been adequately tested, at least in my opinion. I thought that, if I got a better understanding of flow theory and mechanics, it might help us in our vascular work. If I could pinpoint its weaknesses, maybe they could be corrected."

El popped a cookie into his mouth and munched it thoughtfully, silently, for several moments. "You're being mighty careful in your speech, Josh," he said. "It's all right. You can say what you like, and I promise you it won't go beyond this office. You can talk to me just like you'd talk to your minister or, well...your doctor."

Suddenly all the anger and dismay that Josh had walled up inside him over the months at St. Cahill's broke lose and gave way in a flood of excitement. He didn't know why, but he trusted this gentle, sad-eyed man. "Professor, I honestly don't know how much more of this idiocy I can take. I've seen people die hideous deaths because this valve refuses to function, yet the chief continues to use it. He even has me working on a paper designed to promote it, but he's conveniently cooked up some statistics which are just bald-faced lies."

El gazed at Josh, his face a blank. "Sounds serious," he said at last, setting aside the cookie he had been holding. "I should be able to help you, if you don't mind working at night at your own expense. Of course, if you didn't come highly recommended by Hal Frieden, I might not be so enthusiastic. He mentioned you wanted to audit my course."

"Yes, I do."

"Well, of course you can, but you'll find you'll be spending most of your time here in the lab. Let's see...we can construct mathematical models of physiologic systems, but I think what you're talking about really requires a pulse duplicator setup. That's my specialty, you know."

"I know the chief won't be in favor of that kind of system," Josh said. "I mentioned it to him earlier, and he told me that it was nothing but nonsense."

"Well, he doesn't have to know about it, does he?" El said. A smile began at one edge of his lips, worked its way over his cheeks and eventually engulfed his entire face. That was what the man was like, thought Josh: deliberate, systematic, and complete.

"Actually, if this is going to work at all, then Dr. Thornton can't get wind of it. It's got to be kept secret from him, or my neck'll be on the line. He's very much against computerized testing of any sort, a real `old silk line' kind of guy."

"Not to worry, Josh," said the professor. "As I said, nothing goes past these walls. You'll be using my lab, but no one has to know who you're affiliated with or what client you're working for. That's one of the benefits of tenure. If anyone questions your presence, I'll just tell them the truth, that you're auditing classes. Which reminds me, my flow mechanics class meets on Tuesdays and Thursdays at 5:00 p.m. Okay with you?"

"Sure." Josh knew that he'd probably miss dinner, but he'd get by somehow. Maybe he'd buy some Oreos.

Josh returned to St. Cahill's, buoyed by his conversation with the professor. Maybe now he'd be able to really do some good, save some lives, and work with all the fantastic life-saving technology that was just beginning to come into its own.

When he stopped by the switchboard to check his messages, the operator handed him a note: one of Thornton's heart patients on the Gold Coast was in congestive heart failure. Josh rushed upstairs just in time to see the man rapidly deteriorate and die. Josh held the dead patient's hand for a long time. "I promise this won't go on much longer," he whispered to the corpse. "Not if I can help it."

12

Josh spent every free moment at Kingston Andrews with El, either in class or in the professor's lab. Josh was fascinated by the topic of laminar flow, and thought that, if he hadn't become a surgeon, he might have made a good fluid engineer. Together, he and El developed a computer program for the Naviere-Stokes equation, essential for determining the flow of fluids. With a few alterations, El said, the program could be used to model blood flow in the vascular system.

"We can begin constructing the pulse-duplicator system any time you like, though we need to collect some equipment first—tubing, pressure gauges, connecting valves and so on. We'll also need some sort of fluid to simulate human blood...perhaps cattle blood. The pressure measurements are easy to get. You can look them up in a textbook. But what we really need is the Thornton Valve in the flesh, so to speak. Is there any way you can get hold of one?"

"Get you a Thornton Valve?" Josh knew the request was akin to asking for the Golden Fleece. "I'm afraid it's not going to be all that easy. The valve isn't a 'general issue' sort of apparatus. Jack Radcliff, the guy who engineered it, runs his lab like a fortress, and he oversees the ordering of the valves."

"Too bad. Maybe we can create a model of one, based on your descriptions and the diagrams you brought me."

"Maybe. Maybe not. It sure wasn't easy getting those," Josh said, remembering the evening he had coaxed and cajoled a security guard into letting him into the lab, where he'd made copies of the necessary drawings. "I don't think that even the pond scum St. Cahill's calls their security staff would let me walk out of the lab with a valve under my arm."

"Of course," sighed El. "Well, we'll just have to make do.

Having the real McCoy would be perfect, but I'm not expecting you to work the impossible."

When Josh went to the ward the next morning to begin his rounds, Nelson intercepted him before he had a chance to wheel out the charts. "You've been assigned to a mighty important patient in 306." Nelson nodded in the general direction of the Gold Coast. 306 was the largest, most luxurious room in that luxurious facility. "Alan Seidel, Mr. Lake's brother-in-law. Better go visit him stat."

Josh looked through his charts. "I don't see him here. Are you sure?"

Nelson nodded. "Do you think I'm making this up? Why would I want *you* to handle such an important case?" He handed Josh a chart with information on the new patient.

As Josh scanned the file, he remembered the argument between Lake and a man named Alan, the argument he had overheard on his way out of Thornton's office. He quickly tried to dismiss it. If there was bad blood between these two men, he didn't want to know about it. He was a surgeon. He duty was to heal, not to get involved in family disputes...or arguments with arrogant chief residents. "What's he in for?"

"Angina pectoris," Nelson said. "He experienced severe chest pains last night while riding his horse. Took a nasty fall."

"Not a candidate for the Thornton Valve, I hope."

Nelson glared at Josh and shook his head. "Look, doctor, just a word to the wise—the less sarcasm about that valve the better."

Josh hesitated, realizing that he'd made a mistake to let his guard down around Nelson, who was clearly one of *them*. "Forget I said anything," Josh answered. "I just didn't get much sleep last night."

Josh went immediately to Room 306 and was surprised to find Seidel looking alert and hale, despite a cast on his right forearm. Beside him sat a beautiful dark-haired woman in a navy blue suit.

Josh introduced himself, and Seidel introduced the woman. As he had thought, the brunette was Seidel's wife, Sarah. "Well, Mr. Seidel, I must say you look pretty chipper, considering what I read in your chart. You had some intense pain and difficulty breathing, is that right?"

Seidel gave a nod. He was a tall, heavy-set man with receding blond hair. "Yes," he said. "I'm much better now, though. Do you think I can be discharged today?"

Josh looked at Seidel's chart and shook his head. "Sorry, it looks like you'll be here for a while. We have to run some tests and get some data. Then we'll have a better idea of what's wrong and how we can help you." He pointed to a cast on Seidel's right forearm. "Your chart says you broke your wrist during the riding incident. Is that right?"

"Yes," Seidel sighed. "I was cantering my horse in the arena when I had the attack, and I tumbled over his shoulder. Fell right on my wrist."

"It was very frightening," his wife whispered.

"I'm sure it was, but things will get better now," Josh reassured her. He only hoped he was right. Tragic "accidents"—drug misdosages, unnecessary surgery, and flawed testing were all too common at St. Cahill's, even for patients like Seidel, who had a good chance at total recovery.

Josh was leaving when Sarah Seidel stood up and laid her hand on his wrist. "Doctor, may I speak with you in private?"

"Of course. Let's step into the hall. Mr. Seidel, I promise not to keep your wife away for very long." Josh smiled and led the woman into the hallway amid the cacophony of the speaker system and the rattling of carts.

"This isn't very private," she said.

"So it isn't," Josh said. "Let's try the chapel." They took the elevator to the lobby; fortunately, the chapel was empty, quiet and softly lit. "Mrs. Seidel, I can understand your concern for your husband, but I assure you that...."

"Wait, listen," she whispered. Her lean, elegant face, practically free of makeup, was only inches from his. She smelled of the same perfume Becky wore, *L'aire du Temps*. "They're trying to kill Alan."

Josh felt his head rear back in surprise. Normally he would have dismissed such an outlandish charge, but lately he'd become suspicious of everything that happened at St. Cahill's. "They? Who do you mean?"

Sarah shrugged, an odd gesture from such a slender, refined-looking woman. "All I know is that Alan was getting phone calls late at night right before he got sick. He became very upset as he was talking, and he was upset afterward, too."

Josh remembered the conversation he had overheard: *These guys are pretty tough.* Evidently Alan Seidel was mixed up with a desperate crowd. "Did he mention who called?"

"No, but he kept talking about money when he was on the phone with these people," she said, sighing. "I knew he was having financial problems, but I never thought they were this bad."

Josh cocked his head. "You mean so bad that they'd kill him."

She stared up at him, fear glowing in her light brown eyes. "That's right."

"I'd like to help you, Mrs. Seidel, but I don't know what I can do," Josh said, puzzled as much by the woman's need to confide in him as much as by her drastic disclosure. "Perhaps this is something you should take to the police."

Sarah collapsed on a padded pew, a single tear cutting a path down her cheek. "I can't," she said. "Whatever I say to you is in strictest confidence, isn't it?" she continued, looking him in the eye.

Josh nodded, wondering if he was about to regret the existence of physician confidentiality. "Of course, but I have to warn you, if you reveal a crime to me, I may have to warn the police."

"*May* have to?"

"Well, if I determine that going to the police would endanger your husband's health, then I'd stay silent."

She paused, her hand to her forehead, and stared at the deep blue carpeting for several moments. Josh feared that she might pass out, and he put his hand on her shoulder to steady her.

"Thank you," she said. "I have to trust someone, and you seem to be the first honest person I've spoken to since we got here. You see, Alan is...well, he borrowed some funds from his corporation without getting the proper approval."

Josh felt a shiver run though his hands. Like so many surgeons he had talked to, he always felt his emotions in his hands first and his mind second. "He embezzled money?"

"That's such a harsh way to put it," she said. "He never meant to steal the money. He was going to pay it back, after he took care of his accounts."

"How much?" *Damn it, Alan. You've got to pay it back. Can you imagine the bad press?* Philip Lake's angry voice still vibrated in Josh's mind. Josh had dismissed the argument, assuming it was just a family spat. Now, with Alan's wife weeping in front of him, Lake's admonition had a much more sinister sound to it.

"I...I don't know," she said, putting a handkerchief to her damp cheek. "I think it's pretty sizable, though. You won't go to the police, will you?"

Josh patted her hand. She certainly was beautiful, and it was pleasantly distracting just to be in her company, even if she was so anxious about her husband. "No, not while Mr. Seidel is in intensive care. Besides, all I know is what you've told me. It's possible you might be mistaken for all I know. I just wish I knew some way I could help you." He wondered if he should mention Alan's squabble with Lake, then decided against it; Sarah hadn't even mentioned her brother.

"Keep your eyes open, doctor," Sarah said, rising. For the first time Josh noticed that she was almost as tall as he was, five-ten or -eleven. "You're monitoring his treatment and medication, so you're in a perfect position to notice if anything seems out of the ordinary. Just remember, what might look like an accident or mistake could really be something else."

Before he could answer, the woman had turned and left the chapel, leaving him staring after her, his mouth open. Just what he needed, a patient with a contract on his head. He doubted that was the case, though. After all, Sarah Seidel was distraught over her husband's illness; in her heightened emotional state, she could be exaggerating both the nature of the mysterious phone calls and her husband's financial situation. Still, if Alan Seidel were being pursued by some thug, or even a prankster, what Sarah had said still held true. He was in the best position to monitor the situation. And, he was probably one of the very few people she'd likely to meet at St. Cahill's who would be willing to do so.

Sarah and her husband were on his mind all that morning as he went about his rounds. Josh couldn't forget the conversation between Alan and Lake or the sound of fear in Sarah's voice when she spoke about the mysterious telephone calls. He was just thinking about grabbing a quick lunch when Nelson surprised him in a hallway and pushed him into a laundry room. "I hope you don't think you're pulling one over on me," he snarled.

"I don't know what you're talking about," Josh said. Nelson gripped Josh by the jacket, and Josh pushed the resident's hand away. "But then again, I rarely do."

"Save your smart-ass talk for the chief," Nelson said. "You're going to need it when he finds out where you've been spending your evenings and weekends."

Josh stared at Nelson in confusion. "What are you talking about?" Nelson was full of bluff, but just the idea that he could turn into an informer made Josh nervous.

"Cut the shit," Nelson growled, grabbing Josh again, this time by the shoulder of his jacket. "Maybe you can fool Dr. God, but your bullshit doesn't faze me. You're studying fluid mechanics so you can test that frigging valve and become some kind of martyr, maybe present your findings at the surgeon's conference next month and blow this whole place sky-high. Then where would Thornton be? Where would I be?"

"Listen, you stupid asshole, my free time is my own, so back off," snapped Josh, shoving Nelson aside. The man made him nervous; he had such a devious mind it was difficult trying to put anything past him. "Dr. Thornton does know about my classes, and he's happy I'm spending so much time trying to learn more about his valve so I can write a better paper for him."

Nelson laughed, and pushed Josh in the chest. "Oh, right! Can it, Walker. You make me sick."

"It's true. Ask him. Look, if I were to try to test the valve," he said, choosing his words carefully, "then I would be doing it to improve the design, not to destroy Thornton or Radcliff or even you. Surely a defective valve isn't going to do Thornton or anybody else any good."

"It would if you wrote a glowing article about it," Nelson spat, "true or not. But Radcliff tells me your dragging your feet on this paper. Don't worry, wuss. I'm not going to rat on you. But I'm telling you, you'd better learn to cover your ass better than this."

Nelson backed away out of the room and strode off down the hall. As Josh smoothed the wrinkles out of his rumpled labcoat, he wondered how long it would be until Thornton called him into his office. He hoped he'd be able to test the valve before then, or all his work up until that point would be a waste of time.

13

Josh took Nelson's advice and covered his tracks with greater care and cunning than before. More and more he relied on Cantini and Frieden to find residents to substitute for him in the evenings and to invent alibis to cover his absence. In talking with Frieden one night over a cup of coffee in the man's cluttered office, Josh learned that the old neurosurgeon had been running his own tests of the Thornton Valve, using the dog lab at a private facility north of the city.

"Blakely Labs," Frieden said. "They mostly do blood testing, but the owner is a close friend of mine. They're letting me use their facilities; I supplied the dogs myself."

"I know the place," Josh mused. "I used to work there summers when I was in high school, drawing blood from rabbits."

"Blakely is small but reputable." Frieden looked up from his mug of coffee. "Josh, do you know that even Sam isn't aware of all this? The only reason I'm telling you is because I know how passionately you feel about the subject. I don't want to implicate anybody else in my research, in case I find out anything unpleasant."

"Unpleasant?" If he only knew!

"Yes. For example, that Thornton and Radcliff are well aware of the inadequacies of the valve and don't give a tinker's dam about the fact that its use is virtually a death warrant. They know it should be tested and redesigned, maybe even discarded, but since they already have tremendous financial backing from the government, they're reluctant to admit failure."

"So I've learned," Josh said.

Frieden's eyes opened a little wider. "How perceptive of you," he said.

"Thornton told me."

"Well, then...how honest of him. I know he's counting on

the crooked document you and Radcliff are whipping up to bail them both out."

"I haven't written anything yet," Josh said, frowning. "I've done nothing but research."

"I know," Frieden said, running his hands over his graying hair. "You're much too honest to be here, Dr. Walker. You're the kind of person that this hospital chews up and spits out. You've just got too much integrity for the place."

"I like to think so, anyway," Josh said, "but if that's so, what the hell am I doing here?"

Frieden nodded and patted Josh's hand with his huge, wrinkled paw. "I know why," he said, a thoughtful expression on his face.
"You know that being discharged from here could ruin your career. You've got to be careful, Josh."

"I guess you're right," Josh signed. "There's just one thing I don't understand. You told me you were doing tests on dogs, but that must mean you have working models of the Thornton Valve."

Frieden poured himself another cup of coffee. "I have an actual valve, doctor," he said, taking a sip. "Don't ask me how I got it. I'm not proud of myself. But, since I have only the one, that's the main reason the research is going so slowly. We have about 20 cases documented so far. We'll need about 60 or so. Then I intend to blow this whole thing wide open."

"What about my research? Should I continue it?"

The surgeon dumped a tiny bag of sugar into his coffee cup. "Yes, by all means. Maybe you'll get results before I will. At worst, you'll corroborate my findings."

Josh leaned forward. He could hardly believe he had found an ally in this hospital of horrors, but he needed someone to confide in. "I need a valve," he said. "Can you lend me yours, just for a few test runs? It won't take long."

Frieden laughed sadly and shook his head. "Sorry, but mine was just removed from a test case and is being evaluated right now. Even when it's not implanted or being inspected, it's undergoing continuous maintenance, repair and testing. It damaged itself so badly during one case that it had to be completely rebuilt. I suppose if you could wait several months I could get a model made for you."

Josh felt his pulse increase. His breath came short. He had to have a valve! "I can't wait that long," he said, gripping the edge of Frieden's desk so hard his hands became white.

"My colleague is going on sabbatical to Germany in a month. If the work doesn't get done before he leaves, then it won't get done at all."

Frieden stirred his coffee and shot Josh a telling look.

"Elberkann, eh? A good man. Hope they're treating him well at the university."

Josh started, then cursed himself silently. Of course Frieden would know about The Khan! Frieden himself had written Josh a letter of recommendation. "Do I have any chance at all of getting a valve?"

"Sure," said the surgeon, "if you don't mind playing James Bond. Radcliff keeps his working prototype locked up in his lab, in what he calls his `experimental storeroom,' along with all his other crazy gadgets. I'm not even sure it would be missed if you did manage to...um...liberate it, but it's not going to be easy to get in. Radcliff is the only one with the combination to the lock, and I know that the place is rigged with an alarm. What a fanatic, huh? As if his gizmos are worth taking! Wait, this might help you."

Frieden reached into a desk drawer and pulled out a folder full of papers. "This is all the information I have on the prototype and its storage." The moment he took the papers, Josh realized that Frieden had once considered stealing the prototype too.

"Your way was easier, I suppose," Josh sighed.

"Much." Frieden took a drink and grimaced. "Horrible stuff! Actually, my way was far more expensive." A beeping noise filled the silence of the office. "There's my beeper, Dr. Walker," Frieden said. "I'm being summoned. Do you mind if we continue this discussion at another time?"

Josh nodded and excused himself, slipping the folder into

the briefcase he used to carry his notes from his sessions with Elberkann. "Thanks for the lowdown," he said, closing the door behind him.

The next few days passed without incident. Josh kept a close watch on the condition of Alan Seidel, but the health of the chairman's brother-in-law was deteriorating. His heartrate dropped, and his breathing occasionally became erratic despite the best care Josh and Dr. Davenport, Seidel's doctor, could give him. "It's almost as if some outside force is at work against him," Davenport muttered to Josh one evening, mystified by the man's decline. "I don't understand it."

"What can we do?" Josh said, suddenly afraid that there was nothing he could do for Seidel. The man's health was slipping away for no apparent reason, and Josh could do nothing to stop it.

"I don't know." Davenport ran his hands through the few hairs remaining on his shiny pate. "I hate to subject him to more testing, but I can't think of anything else. Can you?"

Josh had no answers. He thought of Sarah and tried to imagine what he could say to her to give her some comfort, but all he could think of was that he was losing his patient. Sarah had trusted him, but he wasn't worthy of her trust.

Josh left Davenport and went to check on Seidel's condition. It appeared to have stabilized. It remained the same all afternoon, though Josh checked on him often. Despite this calm in the storm, Josh knew, unless the situation reversed itself soon, Seidel was a statistic in the making.

Around dinnertime he returned to Seidel's room and found Sarah by her husband's bed, reading aloud to him from The Wall Street Journal. "Mrs. Seidel?" Josh said softly. At the sound of his voice she dropped the book and nearly bolted from the chair. "Oh, I'm sorry! I didn't mean to startle you." He saw right away that she had been crying some time recently, and his heart went out to her. Her eyes were covered with a red spider web of veins.

"It's all right, doctor," she replied quietly. "I...I thought it would relax Alan if I read him something, and this is all he ever reads. Look how tight his face muscles are."

Josh saw in a glance it was true. Even in sleep, Seidel looked as if he were straining to move a mountain.

"Doctor Walker, you and I have got to talk."

"What?" Josh turned his attention from his patient and back to Sarah.

"They're getting to him," she said, walking up to the bed and taking her husband's hand. "I knew it."

"What do you mean?" Josh asked. "Granted, Dr. Davenport and I thought his recovery would be much quicker, but these setbacks do sometimes occur. It could be temporary. Believe me, we're doing everything we can for Alan."

Sarah looked up at him, a stern expression darkening her face. "Do you know a quiet place we can go? I have to talk to you, but not here, not in the hospital."

Josh was surprised by how quickly he answered her. "Yes, but I'm not off duty for an hour yet. Wait here and I'll come by around seven for you." He paused, wondering just what she had to tell him that could not be said in a private hospital room.

Shortly after seven, Josh hurried to Seidel's room where Sarah was waiting for him. A smothering silence hung between them as Josh led her to his car and drove to The Hound and Hare, a British-style pub in the fashionable "Oldtown" section of the city. Walt had introduced him to The Hound and Hare years ago. The pub served huge roast beef sandwiches and platters of fish and chips, as well as an impressive selection of imported beers and ales. Except on Saturdays, when Bluegrass musicians pounded out downhome ballads until the wee hours, The Hound and Hare was dark, quiet and private.

They sat down a booth under a cheerful framed poster for Guiness Stout and ordered beer and sandwiches. "Now, I don't want to be rude," Josh said, "but what the hell is happening? What do you want to tell me, and why?"

Sarah traced the figure of a rabbit embroidered on the tablecloth, then looked into his face. "I'll get to the point. I's sorry if I've put you in an awkward position, but I can't say what I have to say with any hospital staff around. Except you, of course."

"Thanks," Josh said. "I appreciate it. I think."

She gave him half a smile. "Do you know a doctor with very short black hair and a pencil mustache? He has brown eyes and high cheekbones and a full mouth."

Jack Radcliff's face instantly sprang into Josh's mind. It was remarkable how accurately Sarah had described him. "Why, yes. Did he examine your husband?"

"I don't know." Sarah sank back against the bright green vinyl of the booth, and Josh could tell that she was exhausted. A waiter arrived with their beer, and Sarah immediately took a sip of hers. "I couldn't really tell. Just tell me this: Is he a person you'd trust with your life?"

Careful, Josh, he told himself. He hated Radcliff, but he was in no hurry to denounce the man in public, especially to the wife of a very sick man whose recovery depended on the doctors at St. Cahill's. "That's a very strange question. I've done some work with him, but to tell you the truth I'm not that familiar with his surgery. He's very highly regarded at the hospital. Why do you ask?"

"Well, I had to leave last evening and came back late that night to be with Alan. And there he was, this doctor. He was very surprised to see me, and he left in a big hurry, almost as if he knew he wasn't supposed to be there. Didn't introduce himself, didn't explain what he was doing."

"Well, if it's who I think it is, he can be a little eccentric," Josh said, still playing on the safe side. "But I'm sure he wouldn't do anything to harm your husband. He was probably just startled by your sudden appearance. Or your good looks," he added, hardly believing he could be so bold, considering the circumstances.

Sarah laughed and her tired face suddenly became alive and vibrant. "I wish I believed that's all it was, doctor. But thanks for the compliment."

"Did the doctor appear to be doing anything, taking Alan's pulse, for instance, or looking in his eyes?"

She shook her head, and her long hair danced about her

neck. "No, nothing like that. He was just standing beside Alan, staring at him, wiping his hands on his jacket. When he saw me, he excused himself and left."

"Sounds nervous," Josh offered, wondering all the time what the hell Radcliff could have been doing. The doctor did have quite a reputation as a ladies' man, although he was married and had five children. He was also a ruthless, self-centered bastard. Was he a potential murderer too? Josh didn't want to consider the possibilities.

"Maybe. I have no idea," Sarah said, taking a sip of beer.

When their sandwiches came, Josh ate quietly, listening to Sarah pour out her concern for Alan's health and, even more troubling, his safety. Now and then Josh would ask a question or make a comment, but for the most part he was content to look at and listen to Sarah. It slowly dawned on him that Sarah didn't just need someone to listen to her suspicions. She just needed someone to talk to, to trust, to help relieve the enormous pressure she was under.

What she had told him about Radcliff had unnerved him, and he found his thoughts constantly drifting back to the renegade researcher. "I give you my word I'll do whatever I can to help Alan," he assured her during a pause in their talk. "And that includes protecting him from anyone who might mean to harm him."

Sarah nodded gratefully, reached out across the table and took his hand in both of hers. "Thank you, Dr. Walker."

"Josh, please. You're very welcome."

"This whole mess has been very hard on me."

"I'm well aware of that." Josh sat immobile, enjoying the warmth of her touch. It was several moments before he realized he was on the verge of being dangerously out of bounds. Sarah was the wife of his patient, a very ill patient who could be the target of a potential murderer. Sarah was not only off limits, she was in a vulnerable position, and only someone as seamy as Nelson would take advantage of it.

Josh removed his hand. "It's time to go," he said, grabbing the bill off the table.

"Let me take it." Sarah snatched at the check, but Josh pulled it away.

"Ah, I insist. And I'm the doctor, so you have to listen to me."

Sarah gave him the briefest of smiles.

The next day Josh was up early to check on Seidel's condition; it was still stable, and Josh began to think Sarah was just a naturally melodramatic person. The second time he checked on Seidel, he noticed a slight fluctuation in the respiratory rate. An hour later Seidel's respiration was still slightly ragged. It could mean nothing, Josh thought, or it might be a negative reaction to one of the many medicines being pumped into the patient, or perhaps the combination of medications. Dr. Davenport was in surgery; Cantini had been in emergency for five hours stitching up a cardiac victim and was in no shape for a consultation. That left only one competent surgeon in the entire hospital that Josh could trust.

He headed for Dr. Frieden's office late that night after a trip to Kingston Andrews, hoping to discuss Seidel's condition. Though it had apparently stabilized, Josh wasn't about to take any chances. When he reached Frieden's door he stopped dead. All seemed quiet, except for the sound of Frieden's beeper. It was odd: Why didn't he answer it? Maybe Frieden had left the office and accidently left the beeper behind.

"Dr. Frieden?" he called out as he tried the door. It swung open. "Dr. Frieden? Are you here?" Josh approached Frieden's big mahogany desk, following the shrill sound of the beeper. Frieden lay sprawled face-down behind his leather swivel chair, surrounded by sheets of paper, the broken coffee cup and other items which had fallen from his desk.

"Hal!" Josh ran toward the motionless body. He reached into Frieden's pocket, felt around for the tiny turn-off switch and turned off the beeper. Without a second thought he slipped the device into his coat pocket and yanked out his stethoscope. No heart sounds; no carotid pulse. "Come on, Dr. Frieden," murmured Josh, "please be alive." His throat felt tight and dry.

His head spun. Josh looked into the surgeon's eyes. They were fixed and dilated. He'd been dead for some time. Josh checked for signs of violence or self-inflicted injury: no contusions, cuts, burns. Nothing. No vials, no pills, no glasses of water. He sniffed the fresh coffee stain on the carpet, but detected nothing out of the ordinary. The papers on the floor could have indicated a struggle, but he doubted it; most likely they indicated the untidy state of the surgeon's desk.

Josh rose unsteadily, fumbled for the phone on a nearby credenza and pushed the buttons for security. In a matter of minutes a full retinue of hospital staff and rent-a-cops had arrived. Cantini was among the crowd.

"God in heaven, what happened here?" he cried, when he saw Josh bending over Frieden's body. "Josh? God, I told him not to let this place get him down, but...."

"I don't think it's a suicide, Sam," Josh interrupted. "No weapon, no residue of poisonous substances."

"The police will determine that, young man." The chief of security walked up to Josh and began showering him with questions, which he answered as best he could. No, he didn't see anyone else in the office with Frieden. Yes, he knew the doctor, but had just come by to ask him a question regarding a patient. No, he didn't know anyone who bore Frieden a grudge. He briefly thought of Thornton, but the chief had no idea that Frieden was conducting an in-depth probe of the Thornton Valve, and it didn't seem right to bring up the matter. Besides, even Thornton, a tough old bastard at times, would never commit murder. He would be too concerned with his image and that of the hospital.

Josh spent half an hour in the office of the security chief, and another two hours downtown at police headquarters, going over the sequence of events concerning Frieden's death. The police officer who questioned him yawned as he talked, as if he were thoroughly bored with the situation and couldn't wait for Josh to leave.

It was awfully late, long past midnight, but Josh was glad that the police seemed to think Dr. Frieden's death was worth their time. He was grateful the officers didn't detain him too long and dared to hope that they didn't suspect him of foul play. He couldn't believe that anyone had murdered the good old doctor, but found it just as hard to imagine that Frieden had had a massive heart attack. The man seemed in excellent shape for someone in his late fifties and had never had any incidence of heart problems.

That night Josh crawled into bed, his head still thrumming with the horror of Frieden's death. Suddenly he remembered the beeper in his coat pocket. He had forgotten all about it. He hadn't even told the weary police examiner that it was the beeper in the first place which had drawn him inside Frieden's office.

Josh jumped out of bed, fumbled for the beeper in the semi-darkness of the room, and found it. Absently running his sensitive hands over its hard surface, he detected something he hadn't noticed before, a peculiar ridge along the side of the device. Perhaps it was nothing...but then, perhaps it was something. He contemplated turning it over to the police, then worried that the lazy incompetent who had examined him might put the beeper in a drawer and forget about it. Finally Josh put the beeper on his nightstand and vowed to take it to Elberkann. The professor knew a great deal about electronics. Surely he would know what to do with the mysterious little box.

Josh had trouble falling asleep that night, though he knew he desperately needed to do so. The beeper, the scattered papers, the look of amazement on Frieden's face, as if he could not believe his own death—all conspired to keep Josh awake, sweating and turning in his bed. He was used to death, but ever since Sarah had planted the notion of murder in his mind, he would never again dismiss every death as normal. For some reason he couldn't quite fathom, he knew that Frieden's death had not been accidental.

Just when he had resigned himself to a night without rest, Josh found himself out of bed, walking the corridors of the hospital, dressed only in a t-shirt and his pajama bottoms. He glanced around, embarrassed, but saw no one, not even a night nurse. Josh peeked into one room after another, but all the patients were missing, their sheets and blankets in complete disarray. Trays of half-eaten meals lay in some of the rooms, as if the patients had disappeared during mid-bite.

As Josh made his way through the ward, familiar yet also oddly unfamiliar under glaring white lights, he noticed a doctor in green surgery scrubs hurrying toward him. "Doctor, doctor!" Josh yelled, running up to the man. "Where is everyone?" One of the bright lights overhead blinked once, twice. A large dog with a deep wound in its chest walked past, unconcerned, trailing gouts of blood across the gleaming white floor. "Where is everyone?" Josh screamed again, striking the surgeon in the chest with his fists. He had never felt so frightened before in his life, but he didn't know why. Nothing seemed especially amiss.

The doctor removed his mask. The blue tinge of his skin contrasted boldly with the green of his clothing.

It was Frieden. "Josh, I need your help," he said in a calm, even voice. "Many are involved here."

Josh awoke, shuddering, half expecting the dead doctor to be standing in front of him in the darkness of the tiny room. His heart pounded as if a great weight was pressing against his chest, and he noticed that his pajamas and sheets were soaked with sweat. He sat up and breathed deeply. What was the dream trying to tell him? Perhaps it only expressed the horror of the recent events in his life...or perhaps it indicated something else. The dream-doctor had had a message for him—he needed Josh's help. Many were involved. Good God! A conspiracy! What the hell was going on? Whatever it was, Josh was now more determined than ever to find out, for Seidel, for Sarah, for Frieden, and most of all for himself. He knew what he had to do.

The only way he was going to resolve the matter was to finish his testing, and the only way he could do that was with the Thornton Valve itself. There was only one way to get his hands on it: Steal it.

A strange sensation of calm washed over him, startling him, but he welcomed it anyway, embraced it. He lay back in bed and fell asleep at once.

The next day passed at a glacial pace as Josh forced himself to concentrate on his work and his patients, though thoughts of the valve and how to get it never completely left his mind. Seidel suffered a mild setback, then recovered and stabilized. Josh made some inquiries about Radcliff, but no one at the Gold Coast had seen the doctor for some time.

That night in the locker room of the Racquet Club, Josh confided in Cantini. It was almost closing time, and they were alone amid the smells of Campho-Phenique, chlorine and dirty socks. Josh told his friend about the strange dream, the beeper, Seidel's unusual relapses and most of all, the need for the valve.

"I agree, steal it if you have to," Cantini said, unlacing his Nike court shoes. "I'll go with you if you want me, but keep in mind that I'm not a very good thief. I've only tried to steal something once, and my mother made me take it back and apologize to the store owner."

"What was it?" Josh asked, fascinated. He rarely thought of his own childhood, and almost never concerned himself with that of others. Now however, since Frieden's death, all possibilities were open to him.

"An Easter egg dying kit," Cantini muttered. "59 cents. I was seven years old. I felt like Lex Luger or something. Damn it, Walker! I can't believe Frieden's dead. I wish he'd told me about the research he was doing. Are you sure there's a connection between his death and his research? Damn it, what am I saying? Anything's possible in this hellhole, even murder."

Josh slipped out of his sweat-soaked Notre Dame T-shirt. "All I know is that I've got to test that valve and get everything out in the open before anyone else dies. I don't think Thornton is involved, but what about Radcliff and Ravis?"

"What about 'em?" Cantini asked, stuffing his reeking clothes into his gym bag.

"The other night Sarah told me how she had surprised Radcliff in Alan's room. What good reason could he possibly have for being there?"

"Paying his respects?"

Josh snorted. "You know as well as I do that Radcliff doesn't respect anyone but himself. He and that weasel, Ravis, would do anything to inflate their egos and cover their butts."

"Damn right," Cantini said. "That's why I feel so nervous about breaking into Radcliff's lab. What if he's rigged some sort of explosive device to protect his precious junk?"

Josh chuckled at the thought of Radcliff booby-trapping his lab like some sort of deranged Wile E. Coyote.

"You laugh," snorted Cantini, "but the guy is nuts."

"Right," Josh said with a nod. "That's why we're not breaking into his lab."

Cantini pointed wildly to the papers and diagrams that Frieden had given Josh. "But...but then why did you bring these? I thought...."

"We've got to get out of here," Josh said, buttoning his shirt, "before they throw us out. Sure, at first I thought we had no choice, that we had to use Radcliff's prototype. But now I've changed my mind. We do have a choice."

"What?" Cantini glanced at Josh sideways, as if he thought his friend might spring on him suddenly. "What choice?"

"Frieden's valve," Josh said quietly. "We're going to use his valve. Come on, I need to make a phone call. If we're actually going to do this, we need professional help, and I know just where to get it."

Late that night Josh and Cantini drove to the deserted parking lot of Blakely Labs. The building was just as Josh remembered it from his teenage summers: cramped, squat, red brick, ringed by a pathetic boxwood hedge that was no higher or fuller than when Josh had been working there. Blakely Labs had no guards, but was protected by a full range of alarms and security devices. Josh knew only one person who had a prayer of getting past them.

Walt was already waiting in the lot, sitting astride his big chopper and wearing his black leather jacket and black cotton gloves. An Irish walking cap perched at an angle on his head, ridiculously out of place. "My new girlfriend gave it to me," he said, touching his cap. "Fits right under my helmet. Bitchin', huh?"

"Absolutely," Josh mumbled, shaking his head. "It's you. Dating some lovely colleen, I see."

"Nah," Walt sighed. "Tammy's Polish. She works at the Celtic Crafts Center in Soho. I think it, you know, looks sophisticated."

Josh smiled at the thought of a Walt who cared about sophistication.

"Can we get on with this?" Cantini shuffled from one foot to the other.

"Got your stuff?" Josh asked.

"Right here." Walt hefted a black backpack from his shoulder and gave it an affectionate pat. "You going to introduce me to your friend?" He stretched out his hand toward Cantini, and he and the doctor shook hands.

"Walt, Sam. Sam, Walt," Josh said. "Sophisticated enough for you?"

The three of them walked toward the building. As small as it was, it looked strangely formidable and imposing in the moonlight, and Josh felt his courage begin to waver. If it hadn't been for Walt, he might have packed it in right then and there.

"Piece of cake," Walt said, whipping a can of spray paint from his backpack. He stepped up to a surveillance camera mounted on the wall and blacked it out with the spray. "Hurry." He sprayed a small hole in the side of the door. "Motion sensor," he explained. Digging into his pack, he removed a can with a long nozzle and proceeded to pump some sort of liquid into the side of the locked door, exactly where Josh thought the locking mechanism might be. "Breaks the bolt," Walt explained. Josh heard a loud snap, and Walt pushed open the door with ease. "Wait. Do what I do." Walt lifted his leg in a high, exaggerated step over the threshold. "Another motion sensor. Like I said, a piece of cake."

Inside, he sprayed another camera lens and disconnected an alarm made to look like a light switch.

"You're pretty good at this," Cantini told Walt, his voice hushed with admiration.

"Save the praise for later," Josh whispered. "Frieden said the valve was being examined. That means it's in the shop. I know where it is, but we'll have to go past the large animal cages. Frieden might still have some dogs in there."

"Any other way?" Cantini asked.

Josh shook his head. "There probably is, but I can't recall it. This is the most direct way."

"It's okay," Walt said, his expression full of swagger. "I can handle dogs."

Josh had no idea what Walt meant but realized that he'd find out soon enough. Any dogs used for Frieden's experiments would probably be in no condition to raise much of a ruckus. He led the way down a hall and into a dark room that smelled faintly of meat and ammonia. Cantini reached for the light switch, but Walt grabbed his wrist and stopped him. "No lights," he hissed.

As they entered, several dogs sprang to their feet and began barking, but stopped almost immediately. Walt pulled some beef jerky out of his backpack and gave it to the persistent troublemakers. All stopped but one, a huge black rottweiler with a thunderous voice. The dog's furious barking echoed off the wall and ceiling and excited the other animals.

Cantini clenched his fists and glanced around the room, as if expecting guards to suddenly materialize. "Can you shut him up, Walt?" Josh said. "Someone might hear him, and he's driving Sam crazy."

Walt stood in thought for a moment, then took off one black glove and poked it through the bars of the rottweiler's cage. The dog sniffed the glove, then stood absolutely still, his nose buried in the cotton fabric.

"What the hell was that?" Josh said.

"My dog Sheba," Walt explained. "I petted her before I left the house. She's in heat."

"Fascinating. Can we please get on with this?" urged Cantini. Josh knew he was nervous about being found out. Being arrested for a break-in would mean the end of both their medical careers.

Josh raced to the shop, Walt and Cantini at his heels. Josh showed Walt the metal cabinet where the clients' equipment was kept. An imposing combination lock barred their way. "Are you going to pick it?"

"Hell, no! You've been watching too much TV." Walt covered the lock with freon, then sat back on his haunches and waited. After a moment, Josh heard a snapping sound and saw the lock crack into three pieces. While Walt slipped the fragments into his pack, Josh examined the cabinet. His felt his face grow warm with victory when he saw the Thornton Valve, in a clear plastic box. There was no mistaking its sleek, distinctive design. "Too bad it doesn't work as good as it looks," Josh whispered.

"Yes," Cantini shot back, "then I wouldn't be sitting here on the verge of cardiac arrest."

Josh grabbed the valve, stuffed it into Walt's pack and waited while Walt shut the cabinet and secured it with one of the many locks he'd brought with him. "Not an exact match," he said, "but it should fool people for a while."

At the door to the dog lab, Josh stiffened. A sound that might have been a footstep caught his attention, and he grabbed Walt's arm. "Hear it?" he whispered, his voice suddenly hoarse.

Cantini's face went white, but Walt was unfazed. "No problem," he said, opening the door and entering the lab. Inside, Josh saw the black rottweiler, standing in the middle of his cage, a goofy look on his face, the glove in his mouth. He dropped the glove on the floor, where it fell with a *slap*, just like the sound of a shoe on cement. Then the dog picked up the glove and repeated the action over and over. "They go bonkers when they're in love," said Walt. All three hurried outside.

In the safety of Cantini's car, Josh glanced at his watch. They had begun at 2:46; it was just 2:50. He sighed and felt the terror seep from his body. The most anxious four minutes of his life—so far, in any case—were over. And he had the valve.

14

For days, Josh divided every spare moment he had between The Khan's lab at the university and Radcliff's lab at the hospital. He'd consult with Radcliff, objecting to dozens of minor errors in the article in an effort to slow the project down as much as possible. Afterwards he'd drive to Kingston Andrews. The professor promised to have the beeper examined, but he was more concerned with setting up a system of pumps, reservoirs and pressure gauges for testing the valve. "What we really need is a computer model," Elberkann said one evening, "but it will take a long time to devise an adequate program. This system will have to do if you want results before that conference of yours in April."

"Absolutely," Josh said. "If there's a problem, I'll have to tell Thornton. Maybe I can get him to present the results at the conference, though he's not going to be happy when he finds out that I have proof showing the valve has to be redesigned."

Elberkann shook his head. "I can't imagine he'd be so candid," he said. "I'd think he'd want to destroy the results, not flaunt them."

Late that night Josh and Elberkann finally got their pulse duplicator system up and running. Josh watched intently as the valve's pistons began to pump the cow's blood they were using as a test material. Josh was always fascinated by the nature of fluid mechanics, but at that moment he was more interested in the results than the process.

As the pressure built up in the system, the reservoir nearest the valve started enlarging: the valve wasn't working. "Something's wrong. Let's scrub this test," Elberkann said.

"No," Josh replied. "God, the valve doesn't even function at normal vascular pressures. Try the system with double the head pressures."

As the pressure increased, the blood began to flow slowly through the leaflets of the valve. As Josh watched, he noticed that the leaflets rotated at an odd angle, producing a swishing sound as fluid passed through the valve.

"Holy hell!" cried the professor. "No wonder the valve never worked. That turbulence is terrible, and at twice normal heart pressure, at that. This valve would never work, even in a normal heart, forget a damaged one."

Josh stared at the professor. "El, I've got to show this data to Thornton, the sooner the better, before anyone else is exposed to this monstrosity. It has to be presented at the conference, too. The only hope for the valve is a more streamlined design."

Josh and Elberkann ran the experiment again, with the same dismal results. By then it was past midnight, and both men were exhausted. It was all Josh could do to drag himself to his car and start the engine, but by the time he returned to St. Cahill's and parked in the garage, he was electrified by fear and excitement. Running off with the valve had been stupid but necessary, and presenting his new information to Thornton would be dangerous, stupid, and necessary. He might lose his residency, but he had no choice. He could not, would not watch any more heart patients put through a grueling, needless procedure that offered no hope whatsoever, only to die a grisly death.

He reached his room and had just entered it when he saw that someone was lying on his bed, stirring memories of Lois and Nelson. But this person was clothed...and alone. "Hey, Walker. Guess you're not a wuss after all."

It was Nelson.

"What do you mean?" Josh asked. He knew he wasn't fooling Nelson, but he could stall for time to think.

"Are you kidding? Blakely Labs was broken into a day ago. Nothing stolen...*except* for Dr. Thornton's valve. You're testing it, aren't you? Probably rigged something up at that lab at Kingston Andrews. Hey, it's all conjecture, but it's true, isn't it true?" Nelson clasped his hands behind his head and smiled.

Josh stared at Nelson, trying to suppress all emotion.

"Don't give me the innocent look. I know the truth. If

Thornton finds out, of course, he'll fire you on the spot. Then what are you going to do?"

"Assuming for a moment what you say is true and Thornton does fire me, no big sweat. I'd manage somehow."

"Yeah, right." Nelson laughed, a downright nasty sound.

Josh wiped the sweat from his forehead with the back of his sleeve. Nelson's attitude had always irritated him; now it was infuriating him. "The valve doesn't work. At all. If you were any sort of doctor then you would already know that."

"Too bad you can't tell that to Thornton," Nelson drawled. "I'd love to see the expression on his face when you tell him that his precious Thornton Valve is a piece of shit."

"I already did, and hell, he agreed."

The chief resident sat up and glared at Josh. "Yeah, but you've gone and proved it. That's different. I promise you, if you talk to Thornton about that valve now, they'll be fishing pieces of you out of the Ohio for the next year or so."

"There is no way that I'm letting the hospital staff implant that device in one more patient," Josh said firmly. His voice was steady, but he felt himself trembling inside like a frightened child. "It's morally wrong, and you know that as well as I do."

Nelson sighed. "Well, of course I do, and if anyone ever found out about the valve, I'd be charged with collusion." He rose from the bed and eased toward the door. "I don't want that to happen. Understand?"

"Are you threatening me?"

"Yes," Nelson said. "Listen...the chief's out of town for a while. He may not even make the meeting. If you insist on being crazy, doctor, then go ahead and tell him. But like I told you before, you mess with my reputation and you're in trouble. And so is Cantini." Like a shadow, he slipped through the door and was gone.

There was no sleep for Josh that night. Though he was so tired he could hardly keep his head up, he was kept busy by disaster after disaster in Emergency: a gunshot wound, a car crash victim, an accidental poisoning and a little girl with two broken arms. Josh plied the parents for information, but they steadfastly insisted the child had fallen down a flight of steps. "I suspect abuse here," said Josh. "Look at the contusions about her face and on her wrists."

"Could be caused by the fall," Nelson said. "Let's keep this simple, Dr. Walker. Kids fall down a lot. She just tripped and fell. Happens all the time. That's the problem with you, Walker...when there isn't trouble, you manufacture it."

Around 2:00 a.m. Josh returned to his room, still unable to sleep. He knew he had done the right thing in stealing the valve. That wasn't bothering him. What troubled him was Nelson. The man was unstable, and now it wasn't just Josh who was at risk, but Cantini, too, and maybe even Walt. Josh had to admit that there was little that Nelson didn't know or couldn't find out.

Josh had just fallen into a fitful sleep when he was roused by his beeper. Alan Seidel was in cardiac arrest. Josh rushed to the Gold Coast, and by the time he arrived, Dr. Davenport, Dr. Ravis and Dr. Radcliff had stabilized Seidel's condition. They told Josh they had made a decision: Seidel was a perfect candidate for the Thornton Valve.

Josh couldn't believe it. He cornered Davenport in a stairwell. "Doctor, this is strictly confidential, but you can't implant that valve in Mr. Seidel or anyone else. It's totally nonfunctional."

Davenport stared at him in befuddlement. "You must be mistaken," he sputtered. "Dr. Radcliff has assured me that the valve is the patient's only hope."

"There's no mistake," Josh said, resisting the urge to seize Davenport by the lapels and give him a brisk shake. Instead he grabbed the astonished surgeon by the arm. "I'm right."

"Dr. Radcliff quoted me some pretty impressive survival rates. How can you be so sure of the valve's inadequacy?"

"Numbers lie but physics doesn't. That valve's more than inadequate, Dr. Davenport, it's pure crap. I've run some tests on it," Josh said quietly, looking over his shoulder.

"Authorized by Dr. Thornton and Dr. Radcliff, I assume."

"Well, no," Josh admitted, "but as far as I know it hasn't been tested at all, up until now. If you come with me to Kingston Andrews, I can show you the valve in operation. Then you'll see the level of failure I'm talking about."

Davenport shook his head and broke away from Josh's grip. "Too late," he murmured. "My schedule's full, and we're pressed for time as it is. Sorry, doctor. If Dr. Thornton were here, I'd talk to him about it, but without his authorization, my hands are tied. I have to assume Dr. Radcliff knows what he's talking about. It's his area of expertise."

"Where is Dr. Radcliff now, doctor?" Josh asked, aware as he spoke that his voice was shaking.

"He was in his lab earlier this morning," Davenport said, already beginning to walk away. "You can try him there. We've scheduled Mr. Seidel's surgery for tomorrow morning, if all goes well."

"If all goes well, there won't be any surgery," Josh growled. At his first chance for a break from his rounds he hurried to Radcliff's posh research labs and found the doctor drinking coffee with one of his pretty assistants.

"Dr. Radcliff, I need to see you. Now," Josh said, glaring at the surgeon's dark, lean face.

Radcliff wasn't the least bit put out. He set down his coffee mug and nodded amiably at Josh. "Dr. Walker, have you met our new lab technician? Ginny, this is Dr. Joshua Walker. Doctor, Ginny Logan." Josh nodded at the young woman, just barely able to control his temper. "I'd hoped you come by before now, doctor. I need your help with that paper."

"The paper can wait. We have to talk. I'm afraid it's a private discussion." Josh glanced at Ginny, and she immediately excused herself and headed toward another part of the lab.

"You don't have an appointment, do you?" said Radcliff.

Josh shook his head. "Let's get it over with." Frowning and complaining, Radcliff led Josh past rows of neatly stowed and labeled apparatus and into his private office. He closed the door loudly behind them.

"Damn it!" he said, throwing himself into the leather chair behind his desk. "I hope you've got a good reason for barging in on me like this."

Josh considered sitting down, then decided to remain standing. He somehow felt angrier that way, and he knew his anger would help him say what had to be said. "Doctor, I'll be brief and to the point." Josh clutched the back of the chair in front of him. "I understand you intend to implant the Thornton valve in Mr. Seidel tomorrow," he said, as evenly as he could.

Radcliff nodded. "Yes, that's correct. The man's situation is growing steadily worse, and the valve is his only hope."

"No!" Josh shouted, surprising himself with the fury of his voice. Radcliff sat back in his chair as if he had been driven back by an explosion. "You can't use that valve! It's not functioning. It must be completely redesigned."

"Oh?" Radcliff laced his long fingers together and tilted his head to one side, as though noticing Josh for the first time. "And what makes you think so?"

"I've had some tests performed, and they validate what my research has indicated," Josh said, speaking slowly so as to avoid another outburst. It wasn't easy. "The results prove that the valve fails to work, even under twice the normal heart pressure."

Radcliff was silent for some time, apparently deep in thought. "What sort of test apparatus did you use?" he said at last.

"A pulse duplicator system, designed by myself and a professor at a local university." Josh went on to describe the setup in detail, getting the sinking feeling all the while that he was digging himself into some sort of trap. Radcliff said nothing, but merely nodded now and then and fixed Josh with his dark, unbroken gaze.

"What sort of medium did you use?" he asked, when Josh had finished his explanation of the tests. "Human blood?"

Josh hesitated. "No, cattle blood. Human blood wasn't available. But...."

"Well, there's your error!" crowed Radcliff. "In case you haven't noticed, Dr. Walker, we haven't done much surgery on cows lately."

"But in terms of chemical makeup and consistency...."

Radcliff chuckled. "You really had me going there for a minute, boy," he said. "No, when it comes to research, you'd better leave it to me."

Josh glared at Radcliff open-mouthed. The man was trying to stonewall him! "But you know as well as I do that the source of the blood doesn't make a damn bit of difference."

"Doctor, if you're finished, I'm busy." Radcliff stood up and walked toward the door. Please leave, but come back tomorrow afternoon so you can continue work on that paper. We're way behind schedule. And don't forget...surgery on Seidel is at 7:00, so be sharp."

Josh was so shocked by Radcliff's reaction that he couldn't move. Radcliff was almost out the door before Josh finally shook himself out of his paralysis, ran to the door and caught Radcliff by the wrist. "Wait, doctor. This is serious. You can't just brush this off lightly. Seidel's life is at stake...."

Suddenly Radcliff turned with such force that Josh flew back and fell against the wall with a thud. "Let go of me!" cried Radcliff. "Get out! Get out! I've finished talking with you. Seidel goes under the knife tomorrow, and that's that. You have no say in this matter, doctor, and frankly I think Dr. Thornton is being awful damn lenient with you."

Radcliff strode out of the office, almost at a run. Josh watched him go. What a chump he was to think that he could stop Radcliff! The man knew about the valve. Hell, as Sarah thought, he might even be causing Alan's sickness somehow. Whatever happened now, Josh could not depend on Davenport or Radcliff for help. And that left only one source of appeal.

Thornton's office was two floors up. Josh took the steps, leaping them three at a time. By the time he reached the office door, sweat dripped from his face and his breath was coming in ragged gasps. He burst into the door and found Eileen behind her desk, her nose buried in a paperback romance, one hand buried in a bag of potato chips. "What can I do for you, Dr. Walker?" she said, not looking up. While Josh gaped at her, wondering how she knew who had come in, she closed the book on one finger and raised her head. She was a very pretty woman, but just then she looked immensely bored.

"I've...I've got to talk to Thornton."

"Dr. Thornton's not back yet," she said, yawning without bothering to cover her mouth. "Would you like to make an appointment to see him next week?"

Josh squared his shoulders and tried to look determined, although inside he was quaking with rage. "Eileen, I've got to talk to Thornton now. You've got his number, haven't you? Please give it to me so I can call him."

"He's at a conference at the Grand Hotel in Cincinnati. You won't be able to reach him," she said, reaching for another chip as she looked into her book again. "He told me he doesn't want to be disturbed except for an emergency. Next time I call him with messages I'll say you want to speak with him."

"No!" Josh slammed down his hand on Eileen's desk, toppling the bag of chips and scattering them over the desk blotter. Greasy spots formed on the thick green paper. "It's a matter of life and death, dammit," said Josh.

Eileen frowned and tried to scoop the chips back into the foil bag. "Now look what you've done. Please get out, doctor. You scared me, you know. I told you I'd leave a message with Dr. Thornton."

Josh glared at the secretary, amazed that he'd failed to get through to her. He'd heard stories about how well she protected Thornton from the stress and strain of daily problems, and now he could see for himself that it was true. He placed both hands on the desk and leaned over it. He felt his face grow hot with anger. "Give me the number," he growled. "I mean it. Now. I'm not kidding."

She cocked her head and studied him for a moment, not the least perturbed, and picked up a handful of chips. Then she reached for the phone with her free hand and punched some buttons. Josh recognized the number: hospital security.

"Never mind," he sighed. "I'm leaving."

Josh went back to his rounds, checking on Seidel every chance he got. Sarah was at his bedside, thin and wane but amazingly alert, considering the ordeal she was going through. With her there, Josh reasoned, it would almost impossible for someone like Radcliff to slip in and pull any tricks.

Seidel's condition was poor but stable. During a late afternoon visit, Josh was surprised to see that someone had joined Sarah in her vigil. The handsome man was wearing a blue Armani suit and a very phony expression of concern: Philip Lake. He shook hands stiffly with Josh.

"We've already spoken to Dr. Davenport and Dr. Radcliff," Lake said, his voice just as loud and confident as when Josh had met him in Thornton's office. "They are cautiously optimistic."

Something about the man disturbed Josh. On one hand, he seemed worried, but on the other he seemed almost relieved. Though his face looked grim, his eyes were bright and free of redness, so unlike Sarah's tear-stained face. Josh remembered the argument he had overheard between Lake and Seidel, and hesitated before saying anything. He drew a deep breath.

"Mr. Lake, Mrs. Seidel—I'd be remiss if I told you there was much hope. Mr. Seidel's sudden decline still appears a mystery to me, and this procedure is without a doubt still very experimental. We'll do all we can, of course, but if I were you, I'd try to adopt a realistic attitude toward the outcome. As for me, I'm going to do whatever I can to persuade Dr. Davenport to hold off on surgery."

Josh watched Sarah as he spoke. The moment he finished, her faced screwed up in a knot and she broke into quiet sobs.

Lake held her against his chest and glared at Josh. "Doctor! Look what you did to my sister! How can you be so cruel?"

Speak for yourself, pal, thought Josh, certain that Lake was not as solicitous as he appeared to be. He simply shook his head. "Sorry to be so blunt, but I thought you might want to know the truth, at least as I understand it. Believe me, my thoughts and prayers are with Mr. Seidel, and I'm determined to do my best for him. Mrs. Seidel, may I speak with you in private? It's urgent. We can go to the lounge on this floor. I just went past there, and it's empty."

"She's not going anywhere with you," said Lake, but Sarah brushed him aside.

"Phil, if the doctor wants to speak to me, then I want to hear what he has to say," she said, running a tissue across her tear-streaked face. Despite her tears and smudged mascara, she looked elegant and strikingly beautiful.

Josh glanced at Lake. He didn't dare let the man stay alone in that room, not after the threats he'd made to Seidel days before. "Excuse me a moment," Josh said, and went into the corridor, where he found the ward nurse. "Please," he begged her, "stay with Mr. Seidel until I return. I won't be gone more than a few minutes."

His plea impressed the nurse, who seemed to sense that something was desperately wrong. She glanced at Lake pacing beside Seidel's bed, then looked back at Josh. "All right," she said, "but I can't give you more than ten minutes."

Josh nodded gratefully, then went back to Seidel's room and led Sarah to the deserted lounge. He looked around carefully as they entered to make sure no one was within earshot. As she collapsed into an armchair, he turned on the television—a talkshow program with an obnoxious host—just loud enough to mask their conversation, in case anyone was listening.

"I won't mince words with you," he said, taking a seat opposite Sarah. "This valve they want to give Alan—it's a piece of shit. It's unworkable. I don't know just how sick Alan is, but I think he's not as sick as he seems to be. Maybe you're right. Maybe someone is trying to kill him. But if Radcliff tries to implant that valve in Alan, then he's as good as dead. I've tested it. I know how worthless it is."

Sarah stared at him in shock. "Worthless?" she said at last.

"Then why in God's name would anyone want to use it on Alan or anyone else?"

"It's a long story," Josh sighed. "Thornton and Radcliff have a lot of money tied up in this valve, and they'd do anything to prove it works, even falsifying test results, even making up statistics and surgical outcomes. They've got a lot of people here at St. Cahill's over the barrel, and they've been getting away with next to murder. But it's got to stop. And it's going to stop here, now, with your husband." Her took her hands and squeezed them lightly.

Sarah sank back in her chair, her face twisted in bewilderment. "I...we...maybe we should call the police after all," she whispered.

"Maybe," Josh said, "but then the embezzling is bound to come out. There is another way, if you're game to try it."

She looked at him, puzzled but curious. "Another way? What do you mean?"

"Because you're Alan's next of kin, the hospital staff will have you sign papers giving your permission to perform surgery on him," he explained. "It's standard procedure."

A look of understanding spread over her face, making her appear more appealing than ever, and it was all Josh could do to let go of her hands. "And if I didn't sign them?" she said.

"They would not be able to operate. You might be in trouble, though, if you don't have some sort of valid reason." It was hard to concentrate on an effective counterplan with her bright green gaze fastened on his face.

"Like religion."

"Yes, Seventh Day Adventists won't accept blood transfusions, and people of other religions have certain aversions to other surgical procedures. But I think in your case you can simply refuse because the procedure has not been adequately explained to you. When they try to explain, ask to see the results of testing on this new valve. That ought to delay them, for a least a while."

"But that sounds too easy," Sarah said.

Josh began to speak, but another person had entered the lounge, an ambulatory patient drawn by the applause of the talk show. "It won't be," he whispered. "They'll make it seem as if you're consigning Alan to certain death, but be firm. Just refuse. Stick to your guns. It's the only way. I promise." He looked at her, and for a moment could not tell whether she believed him or not. Her expression alternated between fear, distrust and resolve, like a newspaper blowing end over end in the wind. "Okay?"

Sarah's head sank into her hands, and Josh panicked. He glanced at the patient, but she was entranced by the TV. "Are you all right? I know it's difficult," he said softly, patting her shoulder. And not just for you, he said to himself.

At last she sat up straight, giving her long hair a shake that sent faint streamers of fragrance through the air. "Yes, I'm okay. All right, I'll do whatever I have to do." Then she turned toward Josh and gave him such a long, cold look that he almost jumped to his feet. "But if you're wrong, doctor, I swear, I'll take you down myself."

"Yes, I know you would," he said, helping her to her feet. "But whether I'm right or wrong, I'm sure my career here is over. I'm down already."

"Oh my God," she gasped. "You really do believe something is very, very wrong."

"Absolutely." Josh took her arm and guided her toward the hallway. For just a moment he pretended she was free to pursue, but only for that one swift, pleasant moment. "Believe me, if I didn't, I wouldn't be asking you to do this."

15

AFTER HIS ROUNDS that evening, Josh persuaded Sarah to take a break, go home and get some sleep while he stayed with her husband. The hospital had settled down for the night, and Seidel's condition had stabilized again.

Josh scanned the room for Lake. "Where's your brother?"

"He left a little after I got back to the room," she explained. "Said he had an important meeting." She kissed her sleeping husband's cheek, then picked up her handbag. "I sure hope you know what you're doing doctor. Can I pick you up anything?"

"No thanks, I'll be all right," Josh said.

After she had gone, Josh settled into the plush gold armchair she had vacated and was looking about for something to read when he had the feeling that he was being watched. He turned toward the doorway. There stood Radcliff, a stunned expression creasing his lean face. "Walker! What are you doing here?"

"Might ask the same of you, doctor," Josh said wearily, picking up a tattered copy of *Newsweek* from Seidel's bedside table. "I'm sitting up with Mr. Seidel. Just in case," he said pointedly, glancing at Radcliff. The surgeon obviously hadn't expected to find Josh in the room. He may even have been lying in wait, biding his time until he saw Sarah leave for dinner. Radcliff had something up his sleeve. The only question was: what?

Radcliff blundered in, asked Josh a few cursory questions about Seidel's condition, examined the sick man briefly, and darted from the room as if he had been paged to emergency. Josh sat back, exhausted and immediately fell into the half-wakeful, half-asleep state that most residents seemed to function in most of the time. "Zombying," Willowby called it. The warmth of the room and the softness of the chair had almost pushed Josh over the edge into a real sleep when he heard someone a great distance away calling to him.

"Doctor Walker? Doctor Walker!"

Josh forced himself into a level of consciousness that resembled wakefulness. "Who is it?"

A nurse was in the room, her hand on his shoulder. "Phone call for you, doctor. A Dr. Elberkann. He says it's urgent. You can take it at the desk."

"Elberkann?" Josh was instantly wide awake. If Elberkann said something was urgent, he meant it. "Can you patch it in here? It's private."

"Well, I'll try," said the nurse, turning to leave. "Elberkann ...must be from another hospital," she muttered to herself. Josh smiled. A few moment later, the phone buzzed. Josh answered it before it could ring a second time. "What is it, El?" he said, nearly shouting into the receiver.

"Easy, Josh," said Elberkann's gentle voice. "Are you sitting down?"

"Yes." Whatever his news was, it wasn't good.

"Did you hear about Frieden?"

"What do you mean?" mumbled Josh. "Hear what about him, other than he's dead?"

"The coroner's report," Elberkann said. "They claim it was a natural death. Massive coronary occlusion."

"Did they do an autopsy?"

"Yes. They said it was a clear-cut case."

Josh shook his head to clear it of a giant nest of cobwebs. "How did you find out? Shouldn't I know this before you?"

"Maybe," the professor admitted, "but Cantini got to me first. Did you know that someone vandalized his car yesterday? Brand new Toyota, completely totaled. My goodness, Dr. Walker, you need to stay in closer touch with your friends."

"El, my head is spinning," Josh said. "I'm sorry about Cantini's car, but it doesn't have anything to do with Frieden's death." He paused and thought for a moment. "Does it?"

"You tell me, doctor. Cantini and poor Hal were close colleagues. Maybe someone is sending him a message. Does your opinion on the cause of Hal's death concur with that of the report?"

"Well, no, frankly." Briefly he thought of Nelson's threat, then dismissed it. Nelson was always posturing.

Josh sighed, rubbing his throbbing forehead. He never had headaches before working at St. Cahill's; now they were becoming commonplace. "I find it rather hard to believe, given the circumstances, what with the doctor's good health and the nature of the...hey! The beeper! What about the beeper? Did you take a look at it?"

For a moment the line seemed to have gone dead; Josh heard only silence. "El? You there?" he whispered.

"I'm here, Josh," said the professor. "Actually, that's the real reason I'm calling. I and another professor, Bill Weizen from electrical engineering, examined the beeper. We had it x-rayed and discovered that it contains some very sophisticated circuitry and a microchip. When the beeper is 'fired,' the device is activated. This in turn activates another signal system, which gives off some sort of ultrasonic signal. The signal is similar to that used to defibrillate the heart, only in reverse."

"What!" Josh shouted. "You mean Frieden was murdered? Someone intentionally fibrillated his heart with an ultrasonic device?" He could scarcely believe he was saying the words that came from his mouth: They sounded like something from a movie script. "I can't believe it. Who would do such a thing?"

Again Elberkann was silent for a few seconds. "Someone who didn't want any damaging information revealed about the inefficacy of the Thornton Valve, apparently. Josh, maybe you should forget this whole thing, the testing, I mean. Whoever you're dealing with here is very unbalanced and very dangerous."

Josh couldn't believe he was hearing the professor correctly. "*Forget* it all?" he snapped. "Are you crazy? Excuse me, but how many more people have to die before this thing is brought into the open? Alan Seidel is scheduled for an implant tomorrow, and I'm doing my best to see that it doesn't take place."

Again Elberkann paused before saying, "Was his condition unusual in any way?"

"Unusual?" echoed Josh.

"Yes," El said. "Did he appear to be recovering, then suddenly take a turn for the worse, without apparent cause?"

Josh sat up straight on the edge of his chair. "Yes, exactly! How did you know? What are you implying?"

Once again the phone was silent, and once again Josh thought Elberkann had hung up. His voice, when it returned, was bristling with restrained rage. "Seidel might be bugged with one of these devices, Josh, or at least a similar one. I don't know. It's just a guess. But apparently the apparatus is so sophisticated, it can be set for increasing levels of damage, so as to mimic the onset of real heart disease, if desired. It's tiny. It would be relatively easy to design a self-activating model that could be hidden anywhere. Seidel could have been wearing one in his clothing and not have known it."

Josh thought about Sarah's description of Ravis in Alan's room. The doctor might have had time to hide such a device. Maybe it had been attached to his clothes at the time he suffered his first attack. "This microchip...I guess it could be concealed in just about anything, say, a plaster cast?" Josh turned his head to get a better look at Seidel, a thin, unconscious figure whose face was almost as white as the cast on his arm.

"Yes, indeed. Perfect concealment. Almost undetectable," Elberkann said. "Who would think to look there, even if they did suspect mischief?"

"Call you back," Josh whispered.

"Josh, wait! We've got to...."

Josh jumped up and slipped the phone back into its cradle. He lurched to Seidel's side and lifted the injured wrist, inspecting it carefully. Nothing. But likely the device, if it did exist, was planted deep inside. If the device could be activated at a distance, what was keeping Radcliff, or whoever held the controls, from wasting Seidel this instant?

The thought drove him into immediate action. He had to

get his hands on a scalpel or saw at once, but leaving Seidel would put him at risk. As Josh turned the cast about in his hands, trying to decide what to do next, he heard a tinny rattle near the end of the cast near Seidel's fingers. Gently he probed the gauze around the opening, digging his long fingers deep into the plaster shell, into the layers of fabric, until his fingertips connected with something cold and metallic.

Josh pulled a hemostat out of his pocket and inserted it into the cast. After some tense moments probing and prodding, he extracted a tiny pellet flattened on one side. What the hell! It had to be the electronic timebomb El had talked about. Maybe he had caused the damage himself with the hemostat, or maybe Seidel had flung the cast against the railings of his bed in his sleep, crushing the device. In any case, it wasn't working anymore.

"Hello, doctor. What have you got there?"

Nelson stood in the doorway, leaning against the jamb. "I want to see that, doctor. Hand it over. Now."

Josh shook his head. "Are you crazy? You don't know what you're talking about. Someone planted this thing in Seidel's cast. It's an electronic device which stimulates fibrillation of the heart. It's a fucking murder weapon, Nelson! Something like it killed Dr. Frieden, and now someone is using it to try to kill Seidel."

Nelson's eyes were blank and cold. "I said hand it over. Now, before I get mad."

"Hell! You're in league with him!" Josh took a step backward and stuffed the device into the pocket of his coat.

"I'm not in league with anyone, asshole," Nelson whispered, "but I'm going to do whatever it takes to protect my butt." He sighed, stepped into the room and gently closed the door. "Now just think for a minute, if you're capable of such an activity. Let's say you do blow this whole thing sky-wide and expose the valve for a fake and one of our colleagues as a murderer. Then what happens?"

Josh stared at Nelson. The guy was an egomaniac, but even

so Josh found it hard to believe that anyone, especially a doctor, would value his job over the lives of his patients. The thought made him sick to his stomach. "Justice," Josh said simply. "Saving lives. That, doctor, you may remember, is why you're here in the first place."

Nelson laughed and fell back against the wall, feigning helplessness. "God, man, I can't believe you believe that." Suddenly he stood up straight and, to Josh's amazement, opened the door. "Okay, I'll tell you what—have it your way, Doctor Walker. You can win this one. In fact, I never saw you here holding whatever it is, and you never mentioned anything to me about anyone here being a murderer. I'm not getting involved in this any more than I am, but you are. So good luck. You'll need it." Nelson gave a brisk nod, and then was gone as quickly as he had come.

Josh, braced for a fight, nearly sank to his knees. Nelson was backing off. It seemed too good to be true. Maybe he had underestimated the man...or maybe Nelson was running off to fetch Radcliff or Ravis. More likely, Josh realized, Nelson was just running off.

For several minutes Josh didn't move, afraid that any moment Radcliff or even Thornton would burst into the room and...he could not even imagine what they might try to do. The electrocardiogram measuring Seidel's heartbeat gave off a steady, comforting string of beeps, and now and then Josh caught the soft sound of his patient's breathing. Outside the room, the voice of a nurse or the sound of the PA system cut through the calm silence now and then. It was well past midnight, and the Gold Coast was sleeping.

Finally Josh collapsed in the chair at the foot of Seidel's bed, but he couldn't relax. The tiny device in his hand plagued his thoughts, and at last he wrapped it in a washcloth and tucked it into his breast pocket. He didn't know what he was going to do with the thing, but he sure as hell was determined not to lose it.

The next thing he remembered, Sarah was giving his shoulders a gentle shake. "Wake up, Dr. Walker," she murmured. "I'm back. I'll stay with Alan while you get some rest."

Josh roused himself from his catnap and looked around. Sarah stood before him, her face pale and weary-looking, her eyes bloodshot but alert. "I've got to talk to you," he mumbled, forcing himself to his feet. "It's important."

She shook her head as if to clear it of exhaustion. "What? Did something happen?"

Suddenly Josh wondered what he was doing. Telling Sarah about the device he'd found would only drag her further into a situation which was dangerous enough as it was. And what help could she offer if she did know what he'd found? "Yes," he said, then hesitated. "I think so. But I can't talk to you now, I'm asleep on my feet. Let me grab forty winks and I'll tell you in the morning. Did you manage to stop the operation?"

Sarah shrugged, an oddly attractive gesture. "I postponed it, I think. They said they would review the situation and get back to me in the morning. The operation has been tentatively rescheduled for Thursday."

Josh nodded. Under the circumstances, it was probably the best that could be expected. Any day now, Dr. Walker could expect his walking papers. "I'll meet you here in the morning. Early. I know it's going to be hard, but don't let anyone stay in here alone with Alan."

"Why?" She squinted and stared up at him. "Does it have to do with what you have to tell me? If Alan's in even worse trouble than I think he is, I've got to know." Her eyes opened wide and Josh could see the fear glowing in them.

"Look, take it easy," Josh said, "Alan will be all right. It's just important to keep an eye on him now and make sure he stays out of surgery for a while. Trust me, Sarah. I've got this under control."

She nodded, trusting him, and Josh felt like a jerk for lying to her. He did know a little more than she did, but he was about in as much control of the situation as a first-year intern trying to repair a ruptured aorta. For a moment she laid her head on his chest, and he instinctively wrapped his arm around her shoulder, hugging her close. Her hair smelled warm and sweet. A bolt of desire sizzled through him, and he hated himself for it. "Got to go," he said. "Take care of yourself and Alan. Good luck."

As he stumbled to the doorway, he heard her call out softly behind him, "Thank you, Josh. I mean it. You've been great.

He smiled at the sound of his name, turned and managed a brief wave before trudging down the hall. "You look beat, doctor," said a passing nurse.

"I am. It's been quite a day."

Josh dragged himself to bed and immediately collapsed in a stupor. Hours later, when the sound of his beeper ripped him awake, he was sure that he hadn't slept for more than a minute.

Glancing at his alarm clock, he saw it was nearly 5:00. When he called the switchboard, a nurse's quavering voice choked out a short command: "Dr. Walker, you're wanted on the Gold Coast now. Mr. Seidel is in cardiac arrest!"

Josh flew into his clothes, his mind churning out horrible possibilities. Maybe Radcliff had somehow replaced the microchip. Maybe Seidel's heart, weakened by the constant assault, had given out on its own. Or maybe, most frightening of all, Radcliff had simply ordered Seidel into surgery and forced the staff to go along with him. It was a wild idea, but wilder things had happened lately at St. Cahill's.

He raced to the ward, but when he got to Seidel's room the sick man was gone. Sarah was doubled up in a chair, weeping into her hands. "Where's Alan?" he cried, grabbing her by the wrists. Although he didn't mean to hurt her, she give a quick intake of breath and glared at him with sudden anger. "I'm sorry," he quickly apologized, kneeling beside her. "They didn't take him to surgery, did they?"

She nodded, still sobbing.

"Jesus! Did you leave the room?"

Sarah's face twisted, and Josh could tell that she was struggling to pull herself together. "Only for a few minutes. I had to use the restroom...."

Josh stood up, his mind recoiling in rage and doubt. *Damn!*

What might Radcliff do now, or Ravis, if he were involved? He had to stop them, but short of going into O.R. and slugging them in the jaw, he hadn't any notion of what to do.

As Josh turned to leave, a nurse entered the room and stood just inside it. "Doctor! Thank God I found you. You're wanted in O.R. Two, right now!"

"Have they begun surgery?" Josh roared, barely aware how loudly he was speaking until he saw the nurse wince.

"I don't know."

"What...what do we do?" stammered Sarah, still seated behind him. "They promised not to take him into surgery because I objected."

"Yes, but if they perceive the situation as a matter of life and death, they'd do whatever they thought was necessary to preserve life," said Josh. Or whatever they thought benefitted themselves, he added bitterly to himself.

Sarah gave a broken sigh and looked up to him thoughtfully. "There must be someone who can stop this from happening."

Josh felt his mouth sag open but he couldn't say anything. Thornton hadn't returned yet, but Sarah had hit on the answer. The only one who had a chance of stopping that surgery was Dr. God himself.

"You told...you told me that if he had that operation...." Sarah said.

Josh turned and stared at her. Even in her grief, with her red eyes and swollen face and disheveled hair she was beautiful.

"Don't worry. He won't."

Josh bolted from the room at a run, scattering orderlies, food carts and aides as he went. There was only one course of action now, he knew, if he intended to save Seidel's life. He'd tried it before and failed, but this time he couldn't. If he didn't succeed, Seidel was as good as dead. If he did succeed, regardless of whether Seidel lived or died, Josh was out of St. Cahill's for good.

He ignored the elevators and ran up the fire stairs, his heart slamming against his ribs all the way. *Hell of a time for a coro-*

nary, he thought grimly. He should have played more racquetball with Cantini.

Finally he reached Thornton's office and burst inside. Eileen was at her desk—no romance novel in front of her this time—eyeing him like a deer noticing a hunter. Beside her stood Judy Logan, Radcliff's new lab assistant, a stack of files in her arms. He'd obviously interrupted them in the middle of some bit of office business. "I've got to talk to Thornton! Now!"

Eileen blinked, but neither woman moved or spoke. They must think I'm crazy, he thought. And in a way, they were right. "Give me his number Eileen."

The secretary took a deep breath and let it out in a long, tremulous sigh. "Dr. Walker, I can't give out that information. If you don't leave at once...."

Josh came up to her and took her hand in both of his. She made no move to resist, but he held her tightly, anyway. "Eileen, I don't mean to frighten you," he said very softly, straining to keep his voice from shaking. "I just want to stop a disaster, a certain disaster that is going to happen any moment if it isn't stopped now, and Dr. Thornton is the only one who can help. This goes way, way beyond emergency, Eileen. This is bigger than simple life and death. This is cataclysm, catastrophe, Armageddon, the end of St. Cahill's as we know it." He gave her hand a gentle squeeze. "So please put me through to him, okay?"

Eileen shivered, as if she had just roused herself from a trance, and tugged her hand away. "I'm sorry, doctor, but Dr. Thornton gave very explicit instructions as to who should call him regarding emergencies, and your name wasn't on the list. I'll leave a message...."

"You've got to help me!" Josh cried, thumping his fist against the side of her desk. A framed photo of a pretty little girl buckled under the force of the blow and slammed onto the desktop with a loud crack. As angry as he was, he had to admit that Thornton had certainly trained his staff well.

"Get out. Get out now," said Eileen in a quiet tone of voice that caught Josh by surprise and made him stop and stare at her, unsure what to do next. Suddenly Judy cleared her throat and he turned to look at her. He had forgotten all about her.

"Dr. Walker, can I see you a minute?" she said. She nodded toward the door and began walking toward it, the files still cradled in her arms. Josh followed her out into the hall, no less enraged but somehow lulled by her gentle voice, her calm demeanor. She set down the files on the floor, reached into a pocket of her long white labcoat and pulled out a crumpled square of paper. "Do you think this might help you?" she said, extending it toward him.

Josh took the paper. Written on it in a scrawl of red ink was a phone number. "What's this?"

"Look, I'm not supposed to have this," Judy said, closing the office door behind her. "Dr. Thornton called the lab the other day looking for Dr. Radcliff. When I told him Radcliff was out, he got really nervous and gave me this number. I guess it's a private line or something. Anyway, I got very busy after that and forgot all about it until you came in just now."

Josh folded the paper carefully and tucked it into his pocket next to the microchip. "Thanks. You're a lifesaver. Really. My next move would probably have been to strangle Eileen."

Judy laughed without humor. "Don't be too hard on her. She's just doing what she gets paid to do. But I certainly don't want to sit back and let some tragedy happen because you couldn't reach Thornton."

On impulse Josh leaned forward and kissed her on the lips. She drew back startled. "There aren't too many like you around here, you know," he said. "Wish me luck." Josh broke into a trot.

"Where are you headed?" called Judy.

"Payphone," Josh shouted back, half a hall-length away from her. To his amazement, she began sprinting down the hall after him.

"Use the phone in the lab," she panted. "Radcliff's not there. It's closer, and it'll be easier."

Josh nodded. The lab was only one floor below him. He pulled away from Judy, bolted down the stairs and ran to the lab. A tech and an intern stared at him as he rushed inside and began babbling for a telephone. Probably convinced I'm certifiable, he thought as the tech guided him to a small office and pointed to the phone on the desk. Just don't hurt me, okay? the man seemed to say with his eyes. He left without a word.

Josh pulled the paper from his pocket and began punching numbers, his damp fingers sliding over the buttons. The phone rang three times, and Josh swore silently to himself, gripping the receiver like a weapon. It was over, he had lost, Seidel was dead, there was nothing....

On the fifth ring, someone answered. "Hello?" said a woman in a sleepy voice.

Josh hesitated. Had he dialed the right number? He was so beside himself, he said the only thing he could think of saying: "Dr. Thornton?"

"Jus' a minute," said the weary voice. There was a rustling sound, a murmur of voices, and several seconds of silence. Great! Josh told himself, the phone sliding in his grasp. Thornton was a ladies' man, just like Nelson. The speech about abstinence and dedication that Thornton had made to his residents? Nothing more than a sham. Worst of all, Josh, had interfered with Thornton's encounter. It was not the best of circumstances by a long shot, he thought grimly, but he had no way of predicting it, and now he had no alternative.

"Thornton here," said a husky male voice. It took Josh a moment to recognize it as the chief's.

"Dr. Thornton, it's Dr. Walker at St. Cahill's," he breathed into the receiver. He felt certain that, if he spoke any louder, he would break the fragile communications link that bound them together. "It's an emergency. I have irrefutable evidence that someone is trying to murder Alan Seidel. He's scheduled for surgery this morning, and I'm afraid for his life. Please cancel the operation."

Oh God, he sounded like a ranting maniac. This was exactly *not* the impression he wanted to give the chief.

"What are you rambling on about, doctor?" said Thornton, in a bemused voice.

"Someone is trying to murder Mr. Seidel," Josh continued, forcing himself to speak more slowly, "and they are using the implantation of the Thornton Valve as a means to that end."

"What?" The humor in Thornton's voice evaporated. "Did you say murder? Are you implying that one of the doctors is intentionally sabotaging the treatment of a patient in order to kill him? Ridiculous!"

"I can prove it, doctor," Josh said, raising his voice a little. "And I'm virtually certain the same person also murdered Dr. Frieden."

"Shit!" Josh held his breath as Thornton cursed, then barked an order that Josh knew wasn't directed at him. "Get out! Leave! I'll call you later." Josh heard the sound of covers being pulled back, then footsteps and, just faintly, the closing of a door. Thornton's voice, when it returned to the phone, was steady. "You say you have proof, doctor? You'd better be telling the truth. You're making some pretty serious accusations here."

"I know," Josh said, taking a deep breath. He patted the tiny package in his pocket. "Right now I happen to be touching a clever electronic device no bigger than a thumbnail which I removed from the interior of a cast on Alan Seidel's arm a few hours ago. Its purpose is to fibrillate the heart and stimulate cardiac arrest, and it can be activated on command. I know because I found one like it near Dr. Frieden's body, and I had it analyzed. There's no doubt about its function."

"The people who analyzed the device...they're aware of its background?"

"Yes."

There was silence for a few moments, then Thornton spoke in a chastened voice. "Have you taken either of these devices to the police or the media?" he asked.

"Not yet."

"Good, and you won't either, not if you value your residency, Dr. Walker."

Josh wiped his hand on his pants leg before he continued. He was dripping as much as if he had stepped right out of the shower, and he dreaded that he might not be brave enough to say what had to be said. "I do value my residency, but not *that* much," he said. "I'm not about to stand by and let anyone, even a colleague of mine, commit murder. And neither should you. If not for the sake of basic decency, then for the sake of public relations."

"Good publicity is often for sale," Thornton said quietly. "So is silence."

Josh fought back a sick feeling in his stomach. Tyranny was one thing, but bribery was another. "Not with me," he said. "This story will break, doctor. It's just a matter of where, when, in what manner and who gets the blame."

"Is that a threat?"

"Absolutely not." Josh realized he had to be careful to avoid implicating the chief; after all, he was begging for the man's help. "The culprit is Dr. Radcliff."

"Damn him to hell!" snapped Thornton, and Josh could not tell whether the chief was surprised or simply angry. "You've got proof it's him?"

"I know a witness who saw Radcliff with Seidel under suspicious circumstances," Josh went on, "and I saw him searching the cast for the device. Radcliff's the one pushing for the surgery; he just about strong-armed Dr. Davenport into it. Besides, this is Radcliff's field. Who else would have had access to the materials and the victims, as well as the training to devise such a thing? If that's not enough, then it should be a simple matter to trace the components of the device to Radcliff's lab." Josh swiped his forehead with his long, thin fingers. He glanced at his watch. How much time did he have left? Or was it already too late?

"What's his motive?"

"Trying to cover up the truth about the valve," Josh sighed. "If it were made public, that's the end of his career." *And yours*, Josh thought, but keep the idea to himself, since Thornton undoubtedly knew the score already. "Or maybe...maybe someone set him up to this, to cover up Seidel's debts by putting him out of commission."

Thornton snorted. He didn't seem the least surprised about Alan's financial problems. "What do you think?"

"Well, you could simply ask him outright," Josh said. "That makes better sense than my hazarding a guess."

There was another aching silence on the end of the line, and Josh imagined Thornton sitting on the edge of the bed, frowning, gathering himself for a final outburst. Josh glanced at his watch, as if it could somehow help him, and clutched the receiver with both hands. 8:02. Barring a miracle, they'd have begun surgery by now.

"Walker?"

Josh jumped. The power of Thornton's voice caught him completely off guard. "Yes?"

"I've decided to take steps to cancel the surgery. You're right, of course. The valve will kill Seidel, whether he's healthy or not. All I ask is that you hand over the defibrillating device you found to Eileen."

"What?" Damn Thornton! Even in defeat he was struggling for control. "That thing is murder evidence. It has to go to the police."

"And it will. I'll see that it does. The sooner you can get it to Eileen, the sooner she can call me back and I can start the ball rolling for Seidel. I'll call her the minute you hang up and tell her to expect a delivery from you. What do you say, Dr. Walker?"

Josh looked at his watch again. 8:08. What if Thornton did nothing? Josh would have to take the risk. If push came to shove, he still had access to the device used on Frieden. Unless, of course, it had been stolen by now. "If you go back on your word, doctor, you'll regret it. And that is a threat."

Then Josh heard the last thing he expected: laughter. Thornton was chuckling to himself. "You little punk! You think you can to anything to harm me? Why, I could have a story released today on the inadequacies of the Thornton Valve and how its use must be stopped. And I'd be a hero for admitting it! Don't think for a minute that you and your little discovery scare me. I can make you or break you a thousand times over, Walker, just remember that, or Radcliff too, for that matter."

Josh nodded in resignation. Thornton was right of course. "I'll do it right now, then," he said. "And then...then I'll go."

"Damn right you will, fucking troublemaker," Thornton growled.

The line went dead. Josh sat immobilized, the receiver still in his hands. His stomach still felt queasy, and the last thing he wanted to do was to rise from his chair and do what he knew would be his last two acts as a resident of St. Cahill's.

He had to. If not for himself, then for Sarah.

He spied a small manilla envelope in a pile of papers on the desk and removed it. Digging into his shirt pocket, he extracted the tiny black box, so insignificant-looking for something so deadly, and sealed it in the envelope. With a terrible feeling of finality welling up within him, Josh jumped from the chair and raced from the lab, knowing without looking that the lab techs flinched as he stormed by.

WHEN JOSH ENTERED Thornton's office, he wasn't prepared for Eileen's response. "Stay right there, doctor, or I'll call security," she snapped.

"Eileen, I apologize for frightening you," he said, suddenly aware that he needed her every bit as much as he'd needed Thornton. "This is a matter of life and death. I just talked to the chief. Hasn't he called you yet?" Eileen shook her head. Josh fished a tissue from his pocket and dabbed sweat out of his eyes. "He wants me to give you this envelope for safekeeping. Okay?"

Eileen eyed the envelope like a child watching the approach of the schoolyard bully. "You talked to Dr. Thornton?"

"Yes. Please...I can't stay. I promise all this will become clear to you once you call Thornton."

She hesitated. Just as she opened her mouth to speak, the telephone rang and she answered it. Immediately she snapped to attention and gave Josh a piercing look. "Yes, doctor...yes, doctor...okay...all right...I will, doctor."

It had to be Thornton, Josh thought. Who else could inspire so much agreement from a secretary?

After a minute or so of continued affirmation and reassurance, Eileen reached out her hand for the envelope. "Dr. Thornton says it's all right, doctor," she mumbled. "But if this is some kind of trick or something, you'll be in big trouble with the chief, I guarantee."

Josh smiled as he gave her the envelope. "I don't believe it's possible for me to be in more trouble than I am, Eileen, but thanks for the warning anyway."

He hurried to the operating room, hoping against hope that something had delayed the operation. When he arrived, he burst into the room without scrubbing before anyone could think of detaining him and stopped just inside the doors. The surgical team was clustered around Seidel, busy at work. The wilting strains of a Strauss waltz played over the public address system, a haunting background for the surgeons' mumbled instructions. When he noticed the Thornton Valve sitting on the table, gleaming like a sword, Josh sighed and gave a silent prayer of thanks: All wasn't lost quite yet.

"Stop!" he cried out.

"Josh!" One gowned figure looked up. It was Cantini. Josh sighed, happy to see a friendly face. "What's wrong?"

A dozen people turned to look at him, including Radcliff and Davenport. He recognized their eyes above their masks, scowling at him in righteous fury. Had they unwittingly cut Seidel when he'd called out to them? He hoped not, but it was a risk he had had to take.

"Doctor! What are you doing here without your scrubs?" said Davenport.

"Stop this operation at once!" Josh shouted. "Dr. Thornton's orders!"

Josh stepped forward a little, just close enough to Radcliff to hear him say, "He's nuts. Call Security. Quick!" Nobody moved. Cantini shot Josh a worried glance and shook his head.

Josh sidled to the right, putting himself within a double arm's-length of the glistening valve. As he reached for it, Nelson came toward him on the left. Josh recognized his voice as he shouted an obscenity. But Josh was faster. He felt his hand close on the valve and gave a thin cry of triumph.

From nowhere another hand darted out and gripped his wrist. It was a young nurse, short and wiry, with a surprisingly strong grasp that made Josh feel as if he'd caught his arm in a lawnmower. His legs buckled as someone hit him from behind. As he fell, he made a desperate sweep with his free arm, missing the valve but landing a solid blow on the table which held it. Suddenly the world seemed to be shift into slow motion. The table crumpled and collapsed, and Josh saw the Thornton Valve, still in its sterile case, rise gracefully into the air and arc toward his feet. Then he, the nurse and Nelson, his tackler, thumped together and fell in a heap on the hard tile floor.

When Josh untangled himself, he saw the Thornton Valve lying only few feet from him in two parts, its plastic case in splinters.

Sterile no more. He closed his eyes and lay back savoring his success. It was short lived. In a matter of moments two residents had hauled him to his feet. Now he could see Seidel on the operating table, his chest reddened by three inches worth of incision.

Josh was congratulating himself when Radcliff came up to him, so close he could feel the man's breath. "You little bastard! What the hell do you think you're doing?"

"You didn't...didn't get a call from Thornton?" Josh sputtered.

"What are you babbling about, you fucking moron?" Radcliff screamed. Josh sighed. His lip hurt where he had cut it during the fall. He should have known better than to trust Dr. God. Josh had lost, and the knowledge crushed him like a stone.

"Leave him alone!" shouted Cantini, but Radcliff ignored him. The surgeon was still screaming at Josh when the two residents grabbed him by the shoulders and half-pushed, half-carried him out of the O.R. On their way through the double doors, they almost collided with Eileen. Josh saw at once that her face was as white as the pristine tile walls of the O.R. "Where's the mike for the P.A. system?" she asked one of the residents.

The young doctors let go of Josh and pushed him away from the O.R. doors. "Get out of here," said one, then turned to face Eileen. His cheeks were apple-red, and Josh guessed the man was in no mood to dispense information. "P.A. system?" he repeated. "Why the hell do you want to know?"

"Dr. Thornton wants to speak to Dr. Radcliff," she murmured.

Hallelujah! Josh ran his sleeve across his sweating forehead and hastily took back what he had thought about the chief.

"Dr. Thornton?" whimpered the residents, in unison.

"You'd better hurry and help me," Eileen said softly. "He's not in a good mood, and I'm sure you don't want to get on his bad side."

Suddenly the residents burst into action. One grabbed Eileen by the arm as the other led the way to an adjacent room. In an instant Josh stood alone in the scrub room, forgotten by the residents and, apparently, the surgical team inside O.R. 2.

Just what the hell was going on? Josh wondered. Not daring to risk another unscrubbed entry, he paced around the room for some time, then, unable to control his curiosity, he eased the doors ajar and pressed his ear up against the crack. The Strauss waltz was gone, replaced by a barking voice that Josh recognized as Thornton's. The room was silent save for an occasional muttered remark from Radcliff and Davenport.

A nurse came up behind him and stopped his act of voyeurism. "Dr. Walker! What are you doing? You're supposed to be scrubbed up and in there assisting."

"Not any more," he sighed, but stood back and waited, unsure of just what was going to take place next. After a few minutes Radcliff erupted from the O.R. and dashed past Josh without even noticing him. The doctor's face was pasty white, and Josh, as much as he hated the man, was worried for his health. What had Thornton said to Radcliff to get him so worked up? he wondered.

Josh was about to follow him when he thought of Seidel and realized he'd better wait to see how Sarah's husband had fared. Sure enough, fifteen minutes later, nurses wheeled Seidel out of the O.R., and while the man looked fragile, he certainly wasn't at death's door. "Will he be all right?" Josh asked Davenport, who plodded behind the gurney.

The big man shrugged. "What can I tell you? One moment it's 'Do this or he'll die,' and the next moment it's 'Don't do it or he'll die.' His heart rate is strong, though, I'll tell you that, especially for a man with his cardiac history. Excuse me."

Josh watched Davenport shuffle his considerable bulk out of the scrub room and down the corridor. If there was any doubt that Davenport had been mixed up in this murder attempt, Josh discarded it that moment. Dr. Davenport was just as confused as Josh himself.

A familiar form strode past him amid the crush of residents and scrub nurses: Nurse Fenwick. Josh trotted to catch up to her and laid his hand on her shoulder. "Please, stop!" he cried.

She spun around, stared a him a moment and gave him a wide but weary smile. "Dr. Walker! You are quite the hero! And just in the nick of time, too."

"What?" Josh said. Moments ago he had been tackled, showered with epithets and bodily forced from the O.R. Now he was hero? "What are you talking about? Obviously the surgery was stopped."

"No kidding." Nurse Fenwick took Josh by the arm and led him aside as the rest of the operating team swarmed past. "Thornton read Radcliff the riot act in there. I didn't know this, but just before he left, Thornton had told Radcliff to abandon all use of the valve, that tests had shown it to have major defects. At least that's what Thornton said in there," she said, indicating the O.R. with a sideways nod.

"Tests?" croaked Josh.

"Apparently Thornton had hired a private company to do the testing," Fenwick continued, rubbing her sleeve against her sweating forehead. "Anyway, I guess Radcliff was trying to prove Thornton wrong or something. It's his baby, after all. "Personally," she said, leaning closer and dropping her voice to an anxious whisper, "I think Radcliff is history. After this, he doesn't have an icicle's chance in hell of staying at St. Cahill's. Thornton really reamed him out."

"Was he angry?" Josh said, upset with himself for not having heard Thornton's tirade.

"Angry?" The nurse's eyes bulged from her face. "Doctor, he was rabid. Called Radcliff a traitor and an incompetent, and a lot worse that I'm too embarrassed to repeat." She paused to catch her breath. "The only nice things he had to say were about you."

"Me?" Josh said. "Nice things?" What good words could Thornton have to say about someone he'd kicked out of the residency program?

"Absolutely. He said that, if it weren't for you, a tragic mistake might have happened, and the hospital could have been responsible for it. Oh...and he hoped you were happy in your new residency at Boston General."

"New residency?" Josh croak, painfully aware that he hadn't been able do say anything but echo Nurse Fenwick's comments during their whole conversation.

"Yes. Why didn't you mention it earlier?"

"Uh...just an oversight," he said. "Things have been hectic, you know." Damn! It was just like Thornton to cover up all his tracks with lies. He thought briefly about trying to expose the bastard, then realized he was up against a powerful force he could never hope to defeat. Only circumvent.

"Have to run," said the nurse, smiling as she patted his arm. "Thank goodness they stopped using that valve before more harm was done."

Josh nodded, thinking about McDermot and the other men who had died from the implant. "Yeah, thank goodness."

"Good luck in your new job," she said, then turned and hurried down the hallway, leaving Josh alone and feeling completely drained.

17

W<small>HEN HE FINALLY</small> dragged himself back to Seidel's room, Sarah was there, sitting by her husband's side, holding his hand. Her entire body drooped with fatigue, but relief glowed from her eyes like a torch. She really did love Alan, Josh realized. In a way, after all he had been through the past year, it was good to confirm something simple and wonderful, like a woman's love for her husband.

He stood silent in the room, a little apart from the busy nurses shuttling back and forth. The air filled with the quiet, steady beeping of the electrocardiograph. A full minute passed before Sarah noticed he was there. She looked at him and gave him a weary smile and a thumbs-up sign. "Dr. Davenport says Alan is going to be all right."

"Yes, I'm sure he will, too." It was amazing, Josh thought bitterly, how well a person could do without an electronic gizmo frying his heart. Someday Sarah would know the truth, and she'd probably find out sooner rather than later, but just then, at that moment, he could not bring himself to tell her what had happened. If her brother were involved in this, it would break her heart. Just what would happen to St. Cahill's reputation was anyone's guess, but it surely wouldn't be pretty. "I'm happy I was able to help."

"Josh, I have to show you something," Sarah said gently. "It's locked in my car. Can you come down to the garage for a minute or two to see it? Alan will be all right by himself for a while, won't he?"

Josh's head whirled, but he nodded. "I guess I can take a break now," he said, adding to himself, *especially since I'm all but gone and whatever I do doesn't matter anymore.* "Alan is in good hands." What was it she could possibly want to show him?

He walked beside her to the elevator, then let her lead him to the third floor of the hospital's parking garage, reserved for visitors. When she walked up to a black Lincoln towncar, Josh stared at it in admiration. With tastes like that, no wonder Alan had been tempted into liberating some of this brother-in-law's capital.

Light streamed into the garage through a large rectanular opening in the wall, illuminating a green canvas gymbag lying on the back seat of the Lincoln. Sarah unlocked the door, picked up the bag and placed it in Josh's hands. "Go on, unzip it," she said, her face blank and unreadable.

Josh did as he was told, then nearly dropped the bag in amazement. Inside were stacks of hundred dollar bills.

"What...what the hell...? stammered Josh, immediately pushing the bag back into Sarah's arms. "Is this some kind of buy-off?"

Sarah stared at him for a moment, in a daze, then laughed in a weary voice. "Well, maybe, but it's not what you're thinking. I found this bag in the back of the car about an hour ago, right where you saw it just now. Can you guess how much this is?"

Josh couldn't even move his head. "No," he croaked.

"Two hundred thousand dollars."

"Where...where did it come from?"

Sarah shook her head, and it was clear to Josh that the money had baffled her just as much as it baffled him. "I was sort of hoping you'd be able to help me sort out an answer, doctor."

"You don't think I...," Josh began, unable to finish the sentence.

"No, but who could have? Surely there are quite a few doctors here who make a lot of money. One of them might have heard about Alan's money problems and...." She paused and sighed. "Well, I don't know. That sounds ridiculous, doesn't it? A wealthy person forking over a fortune for a total stranger?"

"Ridiculous," whispered Josh. Or maybe not so ridiculous, at least to someone as egotistical and controlling as Dr. God. If anyone would give out hush-up money to make embarrassing patients like Alan fade into the woodwork, wouldn't it be Thornton? The more he thought about it, the more Josh convinced himself that the money couldn't have come from anyone but Thornton. Who else had such cash funds at hand? Philip Lake, maybe? But he had refused Alan earlier. No, it had to be Thornton.

"Any ideas on who might have done this?"

Josh gulped. He cleared his throat, stalling for an answer. If he told Sarah what he suspected, he'd just get her further involved in a dangerous business that could kill her. "Sorry, not at all. Probably a secret admirer."

"Very amusing, doctor." Sarah set the money back in the car and locked the doors.

"Not worried about theft?" Josh asked.

"That's one reason I bought this car," she said with a smile. "It's almost impossible to break into. I know. I left my keys in the ignition once. I had to have the lock removed and replaced."

They began the short walk back to ICU. "What should I do with the money?" she asked. A strange smile, a little sly, a little frighted, graced her lovely features.

Josh stopped walking. What an odd question! "Pay off the nice gentlemen who are threatening Alan, of course," he answered. "You know, those mysterious phone calls you told me about? You'll have to wait until he's alert enough to tell you how to reach them, but I'd try to do it as quickly as possible. No use antagonizing anybody."

Sarah gazed at him a moment, and again he was astounded by how beautiful she was, despite her tear-stained cheeks and haggard face. The crafty smile was gone, replaced by the radiant look of honest gratitude. Her expression reminded Josh of the small cards he had seen as a child in church, cards bearing the exquisitely kind image of St. Theresa, the Little Flower.

"You're right, of course. Doctor. Josh. I just want you to know...well, I was so worried about Alan...." She sighed and gave her head a shake, releasing a cloud of perfume from her tousled hair. "I'm so tired I can't even speak straight."

"No need to apologize," Josh said, laying his hand on her shoulder. Things might have been different, he thought to himself, but now it didn't matter. He was just glad the ordeal was over for Sarah and Alan. "You've been through a lot. You'd better get some sleep."

"I can't," she said softly, "not until I've told you how incredibly grateful I am. You saved Alan's life, and I'll never forget it." She had never looked more beautiful than she did just then. Josh slipped his hand from her shoulder; touching her was too painful. "Everyone here has been so...so business-like, almost rude. Only you. You've been different. Kind. You're the only real person here, Josh." Sarah stretched upward and kissed him softly on the lips.

Josh leaned forward, then back. Every atom in his body screamed at him to prolong the kiss. He broke off and stepped back. He was Alan's doctor. That was all. All he could ever be to Sarah. His eyes smarted, and he swiped his hand across them. He must have been even more exhausted than he thought. "Thank you," he whispered, then turned and walked away from her, leaving her standing alone in the shadowy garage. He reached the elevator, decided against it, and bolted up the nearby staircase, hoping Sarah hadn't noticed the tears gathering in his eyes.

18

"Professor, we've got to take this to the police." Josh realized he was shouting and quickly lowered his voice. Even in the security of his own room, with the morning sun washing the walls in peaceful shades of yellow, he knew he couldn't be too careful. Not only did the walls have ears, they had eyes and noses and mouths that seemed to suck in peoples' secrets and private business.

"I have." Elberkann's calm voice took Josh by surprise.

"What? You mean you reported the device I found on Frieden's body?"

"No," the professor said. He paused, and Josh distinctly heard him crunching something. Probably Oreos. "Unfortunately, that device was stolen from the lab just a day or so ago. No, the report I made concerned the device you said you retrieved from Seidel's cast."

"Holy hell!" There was only one person who could have given that device to Elberkann. "Where did you get it? How did you get it?" Josh gripped the receiver like a weapon.

"Take it easy, Josh." He heard the professor take a deep breath. "It appeared in my office with an anonymous note. My secretary said a young man, possibly a student, delivered it to her."

Maybe a medical student, Josh thought. Maybe Nelson. "What did the note say?"

Elberkann paused again. Josh could almost see him shrugging. "Not much. Just implicated your friend Radcliff and asked me to verify the nature of the device. I turned it over to the police when I was finished analyzing it."

"Radcliff...he's no friend of mine," Josh grumbled. He looked at the suitcase on his bed, removed a bulky sweater and repacked it more neatly. "Have they arrested that bastard yet?"

More crunching was followed by a thoughtful pause as the professor chewed his answer as well as his unorthodox breakfast. "I don't know, Josh," he said at last. "I've tried to get information from the police, but they're not very forthcoming, to say the least. My guess is that they've got evidence against Radcliff for Frieden's murder as well as this Seidel business, but they don't want to reveal it yet."

"No doubt about that," Josh said. "Philip Lake could be involved in this, and the police are going to move very slowly until they know just who gets the blame. They can't afford to make a mistake with that guy."

The conversation began to wind down, and Josh found himself fighting off a headache that ran the spectrum from mild to excruciating in a matter of moments. His thoughts went blank for a few moments until his mind fumbled its way back to reality.

Elberkann was saying something about the Thornton Valve.

"...Release the findings to the medical community, if you agree that I should."

Josh shook his head, then regretted it as a fresh burst of pain flashed through his temple. "No, no. It's no use. Thornton has already covered his tail by now. At the right price, he can get any results he wants to prove anything he likes. He's already prepared a journal article about the hidden deficiencies of the valve and how he was duped into using it, if I know him, the bastard."

Elberkann was eager to keep talking, but Josh had had enough. His head was aching, and all he wanted to do was lie back in his darkened room and try to sleep. He excused himself as politely as he could, hung up the receiver and stretched out on his bed next to his still-open suitcase. He had no idea where he was going or what he was going to do when he got there, but it was still a great comfort to realize that he was done with St. Cahill's. And although he had lost, he had also won.

Moments later Josh awoke. Someone was thundering on

his door and shouting his name. He glanced at his little alarm clock: four o'clock. Had he really slept away the entire morning and afternoon? At least his headache was gone.

"Coming, coming," Josh mumbled as he struggled to his feet, trudged to the door and pulled it open. There stood Cantini, his normally neat black hair rising from his head like railroad spikes, his eyes round and wild. He stood with one fist raised and pulled back, as if he were about to smash it through the door.

"Sam!"

"You gotta come!"

Josh stood transfixed, still half-asleep, trying to understand what had possessed Cantini. He had never seen his friend so breathless and distraught, not even after a sudden-death game of racquetball. "Are you all right? What's going on?"

"You gotta see this!" barked Cantini, gripping Josh by the elbow and dragging him into the hallway.

"Wait!" Josh shook himself free "What's the rush? I haven't changed my clothes in two days and I smell like a dead rat. At least let me take a shower."

"No way! This can't wait." With that, Cantini kicked the door closed with a bang, wrapped his arm around Josh's shoulder and began to propel him down the hall. "Radcliff's dead."

By the time Josh and Cantini got to Radcliff's lab, the entire wing was packed with police and hospital staff. Cantini shouldered his way through the mob, and Josh followed at his heels, arriving at the doorway just in time to see a medical examiner stretch a heavy white sheet over Radcliff's still form.

Josh caught a glimpse of the doctor's blood-soaked face and a shattered hole in his temple. The body lay only a few feet from the desk, which was splashed with blood. The burgundy carpet under the corpse was an even deeper shade of red. Josh had seen dozens of grizzly operations, bleeding bodies and terrifying wounds, and none had ever caused him the slightest queasiness. Now he tasted acid in his mouth and felt his stomach churn like a whirlpool. He had to get out of the lab.

Josh clawed his way through the crowd. He made it to the men's room just in time to vomit into a toilet. Cantini, who evidently had a stronger stomach, was waiting for him by the sink, holding a double-handful of paper towels. "I...I can't believe it," Josh said, wiping his face with the towels. He rinsed his mouth several times to get rid of the bitter taste of bile. "What happened to Radcliff?"

Cantini shrugged. "I heard the coroner talking to a detective. Said it looked like a classic suicide to him. After the mangling he took from Thornton the other day in the O.R., I guess the poor guy couldn't take it anymore."

"Maybe." Josh ran his tongue over his teeth. How he wished he had a toothbrush! Radcliff commit suicide? He didn't believe it for a moment. Was it Thornton, still trying to protect his butt? Or was it Lake? Surely anyone who had no compunctions about trying to knock off his brother-in-law wouldn't hesitate to get rid of a henchman who had botched his job. Either one, the chief or the chairman of the board, would have had the motive and the resources to carry it off. Either way, St. Cahill's came off smelling like a dungheap. "But I doubt it. I think it's more likely he was murdered."

"What? Murdered? What makes you say that?" Cantini rinsed his hands and dried them carefully in front of a blowdryer. "You've been working too hard."

Josh gave him half a smile. "Not any more." He quickly told Cantini what Thornton had said over the phone, though he had the feeling that Cantini already knew.

"Look, I'm sorry about what happened to you," Cantini said, laying his hand on Josh's shoulder. "You've done some great things here in this hellhole, and you sure as shit don't deserve what you're getting. But murder? Who would have done it? Thornton's a bastard, but I don't think even he would be capable of that."

"I wouldn't bet my last dollar on it," Josh sighed. His head was spinning again, and he wished he could go back to sleep. Now that he was finished with St. Cahill's, he felt as if he had just finished running three marathons back to back. "I'm just saying that when the police finish their investigation, they may find more, a lot more, than they bargained for."

Cantini raised one eyebrow. "You know something I don't know," he said. "But please, whatever you do, don't tell me. I've had all the intrigue I can stand for one season."

"Me, too," Josh said. "Actually, more than I could stand."

After a breakfast of tea and toast with Cantini, Josh made it back to his room for a long, hot shower. After he dressed, he surveyed the tiny space he had never really gotten accustomed to and decided he would probably never think of it again. His gaze fell on his shelves of medical books and journals, and he realized he'd need some boxes in which to pack them. For a single second he considered donating them to the medical school, then realized how stupid that would be: He'd learned a lot from those books. If he were ever going to start his own practice, he'd need them.

Josh remembered having seen some empty boxes in the storeroom that morning, when he had gone to fetch his suitcase. The boxes would be perfect for his scant library.

Taking the elevator down to the basement level of the building, he walked down one flight of stairs. The sub-basement was a catacomb of small rooms and confining corridors; The damp, cold air made his flesh ripple with uneasiness. *What a dungeon!* Josh told himself, though he had to admit he had never actually seen such a thing. The musty smell of the place, like old books, useless and forgotten, made him feel sorry for himself, and he vowed to leave the miserable place as soon as he could. It was more depressing than the record room in the hospital.

He entered the storeroom and switched on the lone light bulb. Shadows clung to the cement walls, hiding corners, shelves and alcoves. Glancing about for the boxes amid the piles of junk and neglected belongings, Josh was surprised by the sound of sniffling. Someone was crying in the storeroom ...or else Josh had just discovered a very large, very unhappy rat. "Who's here?" he said, disappointed at the thin, unmanly sound of his voice in the echoing semi-darkness. St. Cahill's being as insane as it was, Josh half expected to see Dr. Thornton emerge from the shadows to confront him. He was not expecting what he saw.

"You son of a bitch," came a strangled cry. Josh heard the sounds of someone moving about and rising, then watched as a tall shadow detach itself from a bank of shelves and walk forward into the artificial twilight of the large room.

"Nelson! What the hell are you doing here?"

The chief resident smiled savagely, and even in the dull light Josh could see streaks of tears staining Nelson's face. "Came to get my things, of course. Same as you, I guess."

"What?" It took Josh a few moments to realize what Nelson was saying. Even then, he had trouble believing it. "You're not leaving, are you?"

Nelson laughed, but his voice was hollow and humorless.

"Actually, no. I'm not leaving, not of my own free will, anyway. You just couldn't keep your pecker out of other people's business, and I knew Thornton had to get rid of you. I expected that. But I didn't think he'd dump me too."

"What did he say?" Josh asked.

Nelson took a deep breath, and for an instant he looked downright pathetic. Then his face hardened. "That was the worst part. He didn't say anything. I got a letter from his secretary, saying my residency was terminated as of today. No explanations, no nothing. Not even a thank you."

"You should thank God that at least you're leaving with your skin," Josh said. "That's more than you can say for Radcliff."

"Radcliff was a wimp," Nelson growled. "He couldn't take the pressure, that's all." In the patchy light, he looked like a wolf distracted from its kill.

"Is that what you believe," Josh said quietly, "or is that the party line?" If anything, Nelson knew better than Josh just how ruthless St. Cahill's top brass could be. After all, he had seen the heart fibrillator for himself.

"What do you care?" Nelson dragged his sleeve across his glistening eyes. "You don't give a damn what I know or what I believe."

"That's not true." Josh caught sight of a big wine carton that would make a perfect book box. "I do care, because we're a lot alike. We both know too much. That's why we're being kicked out. No other reason." He pulled the carton from its shelf onto the floor and noticed two others nestled behind it.

"What?" Nelson's handsome features worked themselves into a sneer of utter loathing. "You pissing, bleeding heart! We have nothing, nothing at all in common. I always supported Thornton. Hell, I was like his son. And you....You just couldn't wait to take him down. I did everything he asked."

Josh fitted the boxes inside each other and hefted them into his arms. "That's one problem right there." Josh frowned at Nelson, and the chief resident shrank back against the shelves as he seemed to realize the meaning behind Josh's words. "You knew all the shit that was going on here. I had to guess at it and find it out for myself. When I did, I uncovered it. True, I made a mess of some things, but that's all for the police to sort out. But you, Nelson...." Josh took a step toward the trembling man. "You were a good doggie. You did what Master said. I'll bet you knew about Frieden, maybe even Seidel. Tell me...was it you that broke into Elberkann's lab and stole that rigged beeper?"

Despite the darkness, Nelson's face turned as pale as fresh hospital sheets. "Go to hell," he whispered.

Josh gripped the boxes tight against his chest. He liked the feel of armor they gave him, a shield, a kind of strength. "I feel sorry for you," he said. "You don't even know enough to realize when you've been given the shaft. Don't think for a minute it's going to end here. You'll wind up with so much blame for so much shit that you'll never work another day in any hospital. You know that, don't you? You're the fall guy here, Nelson. We both are."

Nelson slid down against the wall until he was sitting on the grimy cement floor. "I can't believe it," he said, his voice broken with sobs. "This job was my life. Everything that mattered to me."

"That's the other problem." Josh turned and, after some difficulty, managed to open the storeroom door, all three boxes still in his arms. As he slipped through the door into the corridor, he heard the same soft weeping sound he'd heard when he had entered. For a moment he felt sorry for Nelson, but only for the moment it took for him to remember Dantell, Simon, Sarah and Alan.

Early the next morning, Josh was loading his Volvo with his meager belongings when he saw Walt roar up on his Harley-Davidson. "Come to help you pack," Walt drawled as he ambled toward Josh's pile of possessions, McDonald's bag in hand.

Josh stared at his friend in surprise. "How did you know I was kicked out?"

Walt shrugged. "Little bird named Sam told me," he said. "And then again, there's this." He handed Josh a copy of that morning's paper, already stained with coffee. "The whole front page, and a page on the inside too. I figured something might be up."

Josh shook out the paper and looked at the headline.

ST CAHILL DOCTOR DEAD, APPARENT SUICIDE

Not very creative, thought Josh, but direct and compelling. He sat down on the curb next to the Volvo and pored over the article as Walt waited for him, patiently swigging orange juice and chewing on a McDonald's sausage biscuit. The story was clear and to the point, and Josh was relieved to see that his role in the fiasco had been downplayed. There was only one mention of him, on page 10—a young doctor alerting the staff to Radcliff's unauthorized use of the Thornton Valve.

As he read, things fell into place in his mind and made sense. Thornton swore he had tested the valve and discontinued its use, and had the data to back himself up. Of course, the article did not mention that his "testing" took place after he had bamboozled the state into granting him hefty awards to finance the faulty valve, Josh added to himself.

Lake claimed both Thornton and Radcliff had purposely misrepresented the efficacy of the valve. No grand gestures there; it was every man for himself.

Radcliff was implicated in both Frieden's death and the attempt on Alan's life; the components of the fibrillation device had been traced to his lab and even bore his fingerprints. Of course, he had plenty of motives for suicide, or "apparent suicide."

Josh was glad to see that both Lake and Thornton were being held for questioning. As heavy backers of the valve, they were both under suspicion. Whether or not they would be charged with conspiring to commit three murders and coercing Radcliff into their scheme depended on how well they had covered their tracks. If the police were smart, he thought, they could probably come up with a quite a few other charges, too, probably some that Josh would never even suspect.

The article concluded by stating that Thornton had been relieved of his duties at St. Cahill's pending investigation, and that several board members were already lobbying for his resignation.

When Josh looked up from the paper, Walt directed him to another page. A smaller article detailed the disappearance of Dr. John Ravis, who had not been located as of that morning and was wanted for questioning by the police. So Ravis had been involved too. Josh laid the paper across his knees, remembering that Ravis would do anything for tenure.

"Man, what a house of horrors!" said Josh. "I guess I should feel lucky getting out of it."

"Lucky? Sounds like you made it out just in time," said Walt. He balled up his sandwich wrappers and tossed them into a nearby trashcan. "You were about half an inch from ending up like ol' Radcliff there, or my name's not Waltman."

Josh looked up, startled. "I thought it was Walter."

Walt shook his head. "Mom named me after Walt Whitman. She was just a little confused is all."

It didn't take long for Josh and Walt to finish loading the Volvo: two framed movie posters, a stereo and speakers, a cinder-block bookcase and three boxes of medical books weren't much to signify his life, but they were all he had. "Hardly room to squeeze a mouse in there now," Walt said, surveying the bulging car. "Hope it gets you to wherever you're going."

"Yes, wherever that is," Josh said softly.

"You mean you don't know where you're going, Dr. Walker?"

Josh sighed as he picked the newspaper up from the sidewalk and tossed it onto the passenger seat. As far as he was concerned, he never wanted to hear about Thornton, Ravis or Radcliff ever again, but that wasn't going to be possible. "I'm going to stay with my mother for a while in Cedar Hills while the investigation is underway," he said. "I'll probably have to appear in court, and the trial may take some time, but hell! I've got plenty of time now."

"Going to look for another residency?"

Josh shrugged. "Maybe. Maybe I'll go into electronics. I know a pretty good professor of electrical engineering. Maybe I'll go back to school."

"Well," Walt said, shaking his head, "whatever you do, I hope you get yourself another girlfriend."

Josh thought of Sarah Seidel's striking eyes and hair. "There's no one in particular, but don't worry, pal. I haven't given up on romance," Josh said, smiling. "Almost everything else, but not romance."

"How about motorcycles?" Walt put his arm around Josh's shoulders. "Haven't given up on them, have you? I sure hope you're still up for a wild ride with a crazy man."

Josh laughed. The madness of the last eight months had worn him down, and he had more than enough insane policies, irrational people and outrageous behavior in the name of medicine. Still, the thought of the wind tearing at his face, blowing his skin clean, made him feel strangely elated.

"Sure," Josh said, "but only if the crazy man is you, pal."

* * * *